U0085062

序 言

　　「**五分鐘學會說英文**」一、二冊出版後，我們得到讀者熱烈的迴響。一位住在台北，每天去桃園工作的讀者表示，他利用上下班往返的時間帶著隨身聽，耳聽口唸，目前進步神速，已能和公司裡的外國人交談。還有開車的讀者在車內聽卡帶，效果卓著。大家都認為錄音帶唸兩句英文一句中文的方式，實在是學習英語最輕鬆簡單的方式。

　　許多讀者來信鼓勵我們，稱許我們是「有水準的出版公司」。這使本公司全體同仁感到無比欣慰，推動我們加倍努力，編輯更精良的書籍。

　　在讀者的敦促下，我們日夜努力完成了「**五分鐘學會說英文**」第三冊。希望您繼續給予我們批評和指正。

編者 謹識

⏰ *CONTENTS* ⏰

本書採用米色宏康護眼印書紙，版面清晰自然，不傷眼睛。

1. *It slipped my mind.*

Dialogue 1

A : Oh, dear! 哎呀！
B : What's wrong?
　　怎麼回事？

A : I was supposed to call Jim at six.
　　我應該在六點打電話給約翰的。
B : Why didn't you?
　　那你怎麼沒打呢？

A : I was busy and it slipped my mind.
　　我忙得忘記了。
B : Why don't you call him now?
　　你何不現在打給他呢？

Dialogue 2

A : Bob, did you bring my book?
　　鮑伯，你把我的書帶來了沒有？
B : Oh, I'm sorry. It slipped my mind.
　　噢，對不起，我忘了。

A : You shouldn't be so forgetful.
　　你不該這麼健忘。
B : I know, but I've been so busy lately.
　　我知道，不過我最近一直都很忙。

A : Did you forget your book, too?
　　你也忘了帶你的書嗎？
B : No, that didn't slip my mind. It's right here.
　　沒有，那我倒沒忘記。就在這裡。

Dialogue 3

A : John, you're late again.
　　約翰，你又遲到了。

B : I'm sorry. I overslept.
　　抱歉。我睡過頭了。

A : I told you to get a new alarm clock.
　　我告訴過你，要你買個新鬧鐘。

B : I was busy yesterday and it slipped my mind.
　　我昨天忙得忘記了。

A : You could at least have arranged for a wake-up call.
　　你至少要安排請人用電話叫醒你。

B : I didn't think of that.
　　我沒有想到。

〔舉一反三〕

A : You were supposed to call me at six.
　　你應該在六點打電話給我。

B : I know, but it slipped my mind.
　　我知道，可是我忘了。

A : Why didn't you mail that letter?
　　你為什麼不寄出那封信呢？

B : Oh, it slipped my mind.
　　噢，我忘了。

A : Why didn't you remind me to get gas?
　　你為什麼不提醒我加油？

B : I'm sorry, it slipped my mind.
　　對不起，我忘了。

A : Why didn't you tell me John called?
　　你為什麼不告訴我約翰打電話來過？
B : I was in a hurry and forgot about it.
　　我正在趕時間，所以忘了。

A : Did you give Jim that message?
　　你把那些話傳給吉姆了嗎？
B : I'm sorry, it slipped my mind.
　　抱歉，我忘了。

【註釋】

slip one's mind 忘記；遺忘
forgetful (fə'gɛtfəl) *adj.* 健忘的
alarm clock 鬧鐘
wake-up call 旅館中的服務。可由櫃台的服務生照您吩咐的時間打電話到房間，提醒您起床了。或安排朋友或親戚，依你所定的時間打電話叫醒你，也叫 wake-up call。
message ('mɛsɪdʒ) *n.* 消息；音信、傳話

2. It's a piece of cake.

Dialogue 1

A : What kind of Chinese food would you like to have?
你要吃哪一種中國菜?

B : I'd like to have sweet and sour spareribs.
來一份糖醋排骨。

A : Fine. By the way, do you know how to use chopsticks?
好的。順便問一下,你會用筷子嗎?

B : It's a piece of cake.
那是很簡單的事。

A : How in the world did you learn to use them?
你到底是怎樣會用筷子的呢?

B : I was stationed in Taiwan for five years, you know.
你知道,我曾在台灣駐軍五年。

Dialogue 2

A : Jerry, are you taking economics this term?
傑瑞,你這一學期修經濟學嗎?

B : Yes. I have Dr. Jones as my instructor.
是的,瓊斯博士是我的指導老師。

A : How is he as lecturer?
他課講得好嗎?

B : He's O.K., but a little boring.
還不錯,不過有一點枯燥。

A : How are his exams? 他的考試怎樣?

B : They're a piece of cake. 都很簡單。

Dialogue 3

A : Did you take the driver's test?
　　你考了駕駛測驗嗎？

B : Yes, it was easy.
　　是的，很簡單。

A : What do you mean?
　　怎麼說呢？

B : It was so simple a child could have passed it.
　　很簡單，連小孩都可以通過。

A : Really? I had heard that it was hard.
　　眞的？我聽說很難考呢。

B : No, it was a snap.
　　不，那是件輕而易舉的事。

〔 舉一反三 〕

A : Was the English examination hard?
　　英文考試很難嗎？

B : No, it was a piece of cake.
　　不，簡單得很。

A : Did you have trouble finding my house?
　　我家很難找嗎？

B : No, it was very easy.
　　不，很簡單。

A : Do you think you can win the race?
　　你認爲可以贏得這場比賽嗎？

B : It's a cinch.
　　那是十拿九穩的事。

A : Is it difficult to learn to play checkers?
　　西洋棋很難學嗎？

B : No, even a child could do it.
　　不，連小孩也會。

A : Did you have any problem repairing the car?
　　你修理這車子有困難嗎？

B : No, it was simple.
　　不，很簡單。

【註釋】

It's a piece of cake. It's a snap. 那很簡單。

sparerib (ˈspɛrˌrɪb) *n.* 排骨肉

sweet and sour spareribs 糖醋排骨

by the way 順便一提

in the world 究竟；到底（用於疑問詞之後）

station (ˈsteʃən) *vt.* 派駐

checker (ˈtʃɛkɚ) *n.* 西洋棋

It's a cinch. 很有把握；十拿九穩。

3. *I'm working on it.*

Dialogue 1

A : Did you finish your chemistry assignment?
　　你做完化學作業了嗎？

B : I'm working on it.
　　我正在做。

A : Class starts in twenty minutes.
　　還有二十分鐘就要上課了！

B : I know. 我知道。

A : Do you think you can finish it?
　　你認為你能做完嗎？

B : I can finish if you quit bothering me.
　　如果你停止打擾我，我就可以做完。

Dialogue 2

A : I thought you could play the guitar.
　　我以為你會彈吉他。

B : No, I can't, but I'm working on it.
　　不，我不會，不過我正在學。

A : What does that mean?
　　什麼意思？

B : I'm trying to learn to play.
　　我正試著去學。

A : Better learn fast. The recital is next month.
　　最好快一點，演奏會就在下個月。

B : I know. Wish me luck.
　　我知道，祝我幸運吧。

Dialogue 3

A : Mary, do you have that reservation on the night flight to Chicago yet?
瑪麗，你預訂了去芝加哥的夜航機票沒有？

B : No, not yet, Mr. Jones, but I'm working on it.
不，還沒有，瓊斯先生，不過我正在辦。

A : What seems to be the problem?
是有什麼問題呢？

B : I don't know. I just keep getting a busy signal.
我不知道。對方電話老是佔線。

A : Well, keep working on it.
好吧，繼續努力吧。

B : Yes, sir.
是的，先生。

〔舉一反三〕

A : Haven't you finished your homework yet?
你還沒完成家庭作業嗎？

B : No, but I'm working on it.
是的，不過我正在努力。

A : Do you know how to dance?
你知道怎麼跳舞嗎？

B : No, but I'm working on it.
不知道，不過我正在努力學習。

A : Have you found a new apartment?
你找到了一間新的公寓嗎？

B : No, but I'm working on it.
沒有，但是我正努力在找。

A : Have you quit smoking?
　　你戒煙了嗎？

B : No, but I'm working on it.
　　不，但是我正在努力戒煙。

A : Haven't you got that problem solved yet?
　　你解決了那個問題沒有？

B : No, but I'm still trying.
　　沒有，但我仍繼續在嘗試。

【註釋】

　　assignment〔ə'saɪnmənt〕*n.* 作業
　　work on 繼續工作
　　recital〔rɪ'saɪtl̩〕*n.* 獨奏會；演唱會
　　get a busy signal 打電話時獲得對方電話佔線信號
　　well〔wɛl〕*int.*（表讓步）好吧
　　apartment〔ə'pɑrtmənt〕*n.* 公寓

4. You did a good job.

Dialogue 1

A : Jerry, I was very happy with your presentation yesterday.
傑瑞，你昨天的上台報告好極了。

B : Thank you, sir. I did my best.
謝謝，老師。我盡了力。

A : Well, you did a good job. You had some excellent ideas.
嗯，你表現得很好。你有些很好的觀念。

B : I enjoyed working on it.
我喜歡發表它們。

A : I want you to do another presentation next month.
下個月我想要你再做一次報告。

B : Thank you.
謝謝。

Dialogue 2

A : What a lovely party, Mrs. Jones!
瓊斯太太，這個宴會好極了！

B : Thank you. I'm so glad you enjoyed yourself.
謝謝。你在宴會中稱心愉快，我很高興。

A : Everything was perfect and the food was excellent.
一切都很好，食物也好極了。

B : Thanks. My cook always does a good job.
謝謝。我的廚師一向做得很好。

A : My compliments to her. That dessert was delicious.
　　請代我向她致意。那份甜點真是好吃。

B : I'll tell her. She really outdid herself tonight.
　　我會轉達你的意思。今晚她表現得特別傑出呢。

Dialogue 3

A : That's a beautiful skirt.
　　那件裙子很美。

B : Thank you. I made it myself.
　　謝謝。它是我自己做的。

A : I didn't know you could sew.
　　我沒想到妳會縫製衣服。

B : This is the first thing I've made.
　　這是我做成的第一件衣服呢。

A : You did a good job.
　　妳做得很好。

B : I'm going to make a dress next.
　　下一次我要做一件洋裝。

〔舉一反三〕

A : Were you happy with my work?
　　你喜歡我的作品嗎？

B : Yes, you did a good job.
　　是的，你做得很好。

A : You did a good job organizing party.
　　你把宴會安排得很好。

B : I'm glad everyone had fun.
　　我很高興每個人都很快樂。

A : Nice work, son! I'm proud of you.
　　做得好極了，兒子！我為你感到驕傲。

B : Thanks a lot, Dad. 多謝，爸爸。

A : Tom was promoted to manager yesterday.
　　湯姆昨天升為經理了。

B : He must be doing a good job for the firm.
　　他一定在公司表現良好。

A : Your hair is lovely.
　　妳的頭髮真漂亮。

B : Thank you. My hairdresser does a beautiful job.
　　謝謝，我的美髮師做得很好。

《背景説明》

　　要稱讚一個人事情辦得很好，或是表現得不錯，就説 You did *a good job*. 此時的 job 泛指一切事情。相反地，責備一個人辦事不佳或表現得差，就用 You did *a bad job*.

【註釋】

presentation (ˌprɛznˈteʃən) *n.* 上台報告（外國學校課程進行的一種方式，即由學生準備好一份報告，在課堂中向老師及同學作口頭報告，然後接受大家的發問並共同討論。）

do one's best 竭盡全力　　　*do a good job* 做得好；表現得好；幹得好

excellent (ˈɛkslənt) *adj.* 極好的　　　cook (kʊk) *n.* 廚師

compliment (ˈkɑmpləmənt) *n.* 敬意；恭維；(*pl.*) 致意；問候；道賀

dessert (dɪˈzɝt) *n.* 飯後甜點；在美國為布丁、餡餅、果醬、冰淇淋、乾酪等；在英國多半指甜點之後的水果。

outdo oneself 打破自己的紀錄

manager (ˈmænɪdʒɚ) *n.* 經理　　　firm (fɝm) *n.* 公司；商店

5. *I can't come up with it.*

Dialogue 1

A : John, did you hear me?
約翰，你聽見我說話了嗎？

B : What?
什麼？

A : I asked you a question, John.
約翰，我問你一個問題。

B : Oh, I heard you. I'm thinking.
噢，我聽見了。我在想。

A : Do you have the answer?
你得到答案了嗎？

B : Sorry, I can't come up with it.
對不起，我想不出來。

Dialogue 2

A : The man from the bank is here.
銀行的人來了。

B : Tell him I'll be with him in a minute.
告訴他我馬上就見他。

A : What does he want?
他要什麼呢？

B : Money. 錢。

A : How much money?
多少？

B : Too much. I can't come up with it.
很多。我拿不出來。

Dialogue 3

A : Are you leaving so soon?
　　你這麼早就要離開嗎?

B : Yes, this party is boring.
　　是的，這個晚會無聊透了。

A : I know, and it's really a shame.
　　我知道，真可惜。

B : Why do you say that?
　　為什麼你這麼說呢?

A : Everyone worked so hard to make it successful.
　　當時每個人都那麼賣力想把它辦得成功啊。

B : Too bad they couldn't come up with a better band.
　　可惜，他們沒能請到一支較好的樂隊。

〔舉一反三〕

A : John, you owe me $20.
　　約翰，你欠我二十元。

B : Sorry, I can't come up with it.
　　對不起，我目前沒錢還你。

A : We only needed one more point to win the game.
　　我們只要多得一分就可贏得這場比賽了。

B : Sorry, I couldn't come up with it.
　　對不起，我沒能辦到。

A : Don't you know the answer?
　　你不知道答案嗎?

B : Sorry, I can't come up with it.
　　對不起，我想不出來。

A : We need a good band for the dance.

　　我們跳舞需要一支好樂隊。

B : The committee just can't come up with one.

　　委員會無法提供這樣一支樂隊。

A : This company owes the bank a million dollars.

　　這家公司欠銀行一百萬元。

B : They'd better come up with it soon.

　　他們最好早點歸還。

【註釋】

oh 〔o〕 *int.* 噢

come up with 提供建議；提出；想出

boring 〔'borɪŋ〕 *adj.* 令人厭煩的；無聊的

It's really a shame. 眞可惜。

owe 〔o〕 *vt.* 欠債；負債

committee 〔kə'mɪtɪ〕 *n.* 委員會

6. *Drop me a line.*

Dialogue 1

A : Drop me a line when you get to New York.
當你到達紐約時，寫封信給我。

B : What do you mean?
你說的是什麼意思？

A : You know, send me a postcard.
如你所知，就是寄張明信片給我。

B : Oh, you mean write to you.
噢，你的意思是說寫信給你。

A : What did you think I meant?
你以為我是什麼意思呢？

B : I had no idea what you meant.
我不知道你是什麼意思。

Dialogue 2

A : I'm going away for two weeks' vacation.
我要離開休假兩星期。

B : I envy you. 我真羨慕你。

A : No phones, no alarm clocks, no work.
沒有電話聲，沒有鬧鐘聲，不必工作。

B : Sounds like paradise. What are you going to do there?
像到了天堂似的。你到了那裏要做些什麼呢？

A : Sleep, eat, sleep, just rest.
睡覺，吃東西，睡覺，休息就是了。

B : Well, drop me a line when you get there before you start sleeping.
那麼，當你到了那裡，睡覺之前，要寫封信給我哦！

Dialogue 3

A : Why are you so upset?
　　你爲什麼這麼不高興呢？

B : Well, really! You'd think writing was difficult!
　　哎呀，真是的，寫一封信好像很困難似的！

A : What are you talking about?
　　你在說什麼呀？

B : My son. He's been gone two weeks and I haven't heard a word from him.
　　我兒子。他已經離開兩星期了，到現在還沒他的信息。

A : He's probably busy having a good time.
　　他可能正玩得很痛快。

B : He could at least drop me a line to let me know he's O.K.
　　至少他總要寫封短簡，讓我知道他平安吧。

〔 舉一反三 〕

A : Drop me a line when you get to the United States.
　　當你到達美國的時候，寫封信給我。

B : O.K., I will.
　　好，我會的。

A : How often do you write to your mother?
　　你多久寫一封信給你母親？

B : I drop her a line about once a month.
　　我大約每個月寫一封信給她。

A : Write to me, even if it's just a note.
　　寫信給我，即使一封短簡也好。

B : I'll drop you a line when I arrive.
　　當我到達的時候，我會寫信給你。

A : Do you hear from them often?
　　他們常常寫信給你嗎？
B : They drop me a line at Christmas.
　　他們在耶誕節的時候寫信給我。

A : I received a nice note from Sally today.
　　今天我收到莎莉一封精緻的短信。
B : Oh, I must drop her a line. I owe her a letter.
　　啊，我必須寫一封信給她。我還有一封信沒回她呢。

《 背景説明 》

　　Drop me a line when you get to ~. 或 *Drop me a line* as soon as you arrive in (or at) ~. 是送行時常聽到的話。drop a line 是指 write and mail a note or letter (寫一張便條或一封信，寄給~)。這個 a line 原意是「一行」，表示希望對方給他一個消息，或是保持聯繫；並不要求對方寫很多內容。因此，當你的親朋出遠門，但有好一陣子都沒有訊息，你可以說：He could at least *drop me a line* to let me know he's O.K.

【註釋】

drop sb. a line 寫短信給某人
you know 如你所知；你可知道
postcard (ˈpostˌkɑrd) *n.* 明信片
have no idea 毫無所知；不知道
envy (ˈɛnvɪ) *vt.* 嫉妒；羨慕　　*alarm clock* 鬧鐘
paradise (ˈpærəˌdaɪs) *n.* 天堂；樂園
well (wɛl) *int.* 那麼 (表預期)　　note (not) *n.* 短箋；便條

7. *Are you pulling my leg?*

Dialogue 1

A : There's an elephant loose in the street!
　　街上有一隻脫籠的大象！

B : Do you expect me to believe that?
　　你認為我會相信嗎？

A : Really! It's true!
　　真的！這是事實！

B : How did it get there?
　　牠怎麼跑到那裏的？

A : It escaped from the circus.
　　牠是從馬戲團逃跑出來的。

B : Are you pulling my leg?
　　你是在騙我吧？

Dialogue 2

A : Guess who I just met at the library.
　　你猜，我剛才在圖書館遇見了誰？

B : I have no idea. 我不知道。

A : Only John Smith, the handsomest boy in school!
　　就是約翰・史密斯，全校最英俊瀟灑的男孩！

B : Really? John Smith?
　　真的？約翰・史密斯？

A : And he asked me for a date!
　　他還要求跟我約會呢！

B : John Smith asked you? You must be pulling my leg.
　　約翰・史密斯想要跟妳約會？妳一定在騙我。

Dialogue 3

A : Mary, I'm going to quit my job.
　　瑪麗，我想要辭職。

B : Why?
　　為什麼？

A : I want to become an artist. I'm going to Paris to study.
　　我想當藝術家，我要到巴黎唸書。

B : Are you crazy? We have three children, a home, bills to pay.
　　你瘋啦？我們有三個小孩，一個家，很多帳單要付呀。

A : Those things are not important.
　　那些東西不重要。

B : John, you have to be pulling my leg.
　　約翰，你一定是在跟我開玩笑。

〔舉一反三〕

A : She's never heard of President Reagan!
　　她從沒聽說過雷根總統這個人！

B : You must be pulling my leg.
　　你在開我玩笑吧。

A : We had a snowstorm in the middle of June.
　　六月中旬的時候，曾經有過一場暴風雪。

B : Are you pulling my leg?
　　你是在騙我嗎？

A : The boss just offered me a partnership.
　　老闆給了我一個股份。

B : You must be pulling my leg.
　　你一定在騙我。

A : They just discovered gold in my yard!
　　他們在我的院子裡發現了金子！

B : You're pulling my leg!
　　你在跟我開玩笑吧！

A : My wife just had triplets!
　　我太太生了三胞胎！

B : Are you kidding?
　　你在開玩笑嗎？

【註釋】

loose〔lus〕*adj.* 未予束縛的；釋放的
circus〔'sɝkəs〕*n.* 馬戲團
pull *one's* **leg** 欺騙；取笑；愚弄
handsome〔'hænsəm〕*adj.* 英俊的
partnership〔'pɑrtnɚʃɪp〕*n.* 合股；合夥
triplets〔'trɪplɪts〕*n. pl.* 三胞胎
kid〔kɪd〕*vt., vi.* 開玩笑；哄騙；嘲弄
You are kidding! 你在開玩笑吧！你在騙我吧！

8. Sooner or later.

Dialogue 1

A : Jack's late for work again?
傑克又遲到了？

B : Yeah, I think so. Is he always late?
嗯，我想大概是吧。他老是遲到嗎？

A : Yeah. He's been late for five days in a row.
是啊，他已連續遲到五天了。

B : He'll be in trouble someday.
總有一天他會有麻煩的。

A : If he continues to be late, sooner or later he'll lose his job.
如果他繼續遲到，遲早他會丟掉他的工作。

B : You bet he will. 當然他會。

Dialogue 2

A : John, the faucet is still broken.
約翰，這水龍頭仍然是壞的。

B : I'll try to get to it today.
我今天會試著把它修好。

A : That's what you said yesterday.
昨天你也這麼說。

B : I was very busy yesterday.
我昨天很忙。

A : But it really needs to be fixed now.
可是現在真是需要修一下了。

B : Keep your shirt on. I'll fix it sooner or later.
不要激動。我遲早會修好它的。

Dialogue 3

A : Hi, Jack. Haven't seen you for a long time.
嗨，傑克。好久不見了。

B : Hello, Tom. How's it going?
哈囉，湯姆。近況如何？

A : O.K., but I'm still looking for work.
還好，不過我仍在找工作。

B : Too bad, but don't worry. Something will come up sooner or later.
真不幸，不過別擔心。遲早會找到的。

A : The sooner, the better.
越快越好。

B : Good luck!
祝你好運！

〔舉一反三〕

A : Is he late again?
他又遲到了嗎？

B : He'll be here sooner or later.
他遲早會到的。

A : Isn't my car ready yet?
我的車子準備好了沒有？

B : It'll be ready sooner or later.
遲早會準備好的。

A : Haven't they gotten married yet?
他們結婚了沒有？

B : No, but sooner or later they will.
還沒，不過他們遲早會結婚。

A : Is he still in school?

他還在上學嗎？

B : Don't worry. He'll graduate sooner or later.

別擔心。他遲早會畢業。

A : Hasn't the train arrived yet?

這班火車還沒到嗎？

B : It'll be here eventually.

它終究會到的。

〰〰〰〰〰〰〰〰〰〰〰〰〰〰〰〰〰〰〰〰〰〰〰

【註釋】

yeah〔jæ〕*adv.* = yes

in a row 接連；成一排　　row〔ro〕*n.* 排；列

someday〔'sʌm,de〕*adv.* 將來總有一天；來日

sooner or later 遲早；總有一天；早晚

you bet 當然；的確

faucet〔'fɔsɪt〕*n.* （自來水管的）水龍頭

keep one's shirt on （不動肝火）保持冷靜

hi〔haɪ〕*int.* 嗨！（打招呼，引起人注意的喊聲）

in school 在上學

9. I'll keep my ears open.

Dialogue 1

A : Hi, Sue. Did you graduate this year?
嗨，蘇。妳是今年畢業的嗎？

B : Yes, and now I'm looking for a job.
是的，現在我正在找工作。

A : As a secretary? 當秘書嗎？

B : Yes, If you hear of something, let me know.
是的，如果你有什麼消息，請通知我一聲。

A : Sure, I'll keep my ears open.
好的，我會多留意。

B : Thanks. 謝謝。

Dialogue 2

A : I need to buy a good used car.
我需要買一輛好的舊車。

B : What's wrong with the car you have?
你的車子有什麼毛病？

A : Nothing. It's for my son.
沒事。車是買給我兒子的。

B : Oh, did he get his driver's license?
噢，他拿到駕駛執照了嗎？

A : Yes, and now he wants his own car.
是的，他現在想要一部自己的車子。

B : I'll keep my ears open and if I hear of something,
I'll let you know.
我會留意的，如果我有消息就會告訴你。

Dialogue 3

A : How long to the next town?
　　到鄰鎮要多久?

B : I don't know.
　　不知道。

A : I hope it's soon.
　　希望能快點。

B : Why?
　　為什麼?

A : We're almost out of gas.
　　我們快沒有汽油了。

B : I'll keep my eyes open for a gas station.
　　我會留意找個加油站。

〔舉一反三〕

A : Have you heard of any job openings?
　　你有沒有聽到哪裡的職位有空缺?

B : No, but I'll keep my ears open.
　　沒有,不過我會注意的。

A : Have you heard of any good restaurants in town?
　　你知不知道鎮上有哪些好餐館?

B : No, but I'll keep my ears open.
　　不知道,不過我會留意的。

A : Have you seen the sign for Taipei Station yet?
　　你有沒有看到往台北車站的標誌?

B : No, but I'm keeping my eyes open for it.
　　沒有,不過我正在留心地找。

A : Has he mentioned giving you a raise?

　　他有沒有提到要給你加薪？

B : No, but I'm keeping my ears open.

　　沒有，不過我會注意的。

A : Did you see a small boy go by here?

　　.你有沒有看見一個小男孩經過這裡？

B : No, but I'll keep my eyes open for him.

　　沒有，不過我會留意找他。

《 背景説明 》

　　I'll *keep my ears open.* 和 I'll *keep my eyes open.* 都表示
「我會留意。」其差別是：要用耳朵留意的事，用 ears；要用眼睛留意
的事，就用 eyes。當後面接要留意的事物時，介系詞用 for。當然也可
用於留意「人」，如：*keep your eyes open for* a boy in a blue
sweater「留意一個穿藍色套頭毛衣的小男孩。」

【註釋】

graduate (ˈgrædʒʊˌet) *vi.* 畢業　　　*look for* 尋找

secretary (ˈsɛkrəˌtɛrɪ) *n.* 秘書　　　*hear of* 聽說；得到消息

keep one's ears (eyes) open 留意；警覺

license (ˈlaɪsn̩s) *n.* 執照；特許證　　　*out of* 不足…；缺…

opening (ˈopənɪŋ) *n.* 空缺；缺；機會

restaurant (ˈrɛstərənt) *n.* 飯店；餐館

give sb. a raise 給某人加薪

10. *Could you page Mr. Fields, please?*

Dialogue 1

A : May I help you?
　　我能替你效勞嗎?

B : Yes. Could you page Mr. James Fields, please?
　　是的，請廣播找詹姆士・費爾德先生好嗎?

A : Surely. Could you spell the name, please?
　　好的，請你拼一下他的名字?

B : J-A-M-E-S F-I-E-L-D-S.
　　J-A-M-E-S F-I-E-L-D-S。

A : Thank you. 謝謝。
B : You're welcome. 不客氣。

Dialogue 2

A : Excuse me. Could you help me?
　　對不起。幫個忙好嗎?

B : Certainly, sir. What can I do for you?
　　好的。請您吩咐?

A : I was supposed to meet a friend here at ten o'clock, but I don't see him. Could you page him for me?
　　我本來和朋友約好十點鐘在這裏見面，但我卻沒見到他，你可以幫我廣播找一下嗎?

B : I'd be glad to. What's his name?
　　好的。他叫什麼名字?

A : Jerry Jones. 傑瑞・瓊斯。
B : Thank you. 謝謝。

Dialogue 3

A : Good morning. Miller Enterprises.
　　米勒公司。您早。

B : Good morning. This is Ken Davis. I'd like to speak
　　to Mr. Miller, please.
　　您早。我是甘大衛,請幫我接米勒先生。

A : Oh, hello, Mr. Davis. I'm sorry, but Mr. Miller
　　just stepped out of the office.
　　喂,大衛先生。真抱歉,米勒先生剛離開辦公室。

B : Would it be possible to have him paged?
　　可以廣播叫他嗎?

A : Yes. Can you hold?
　　好的。請您等一下好嗎?

B : Yes. Thank you.
　　好,謝謝。

〔舉一反三〕

A : Would you page Dr. Johnson, please?
　　請廣播找強森大夫好嗎?

B : Certainly, sir.
　　好的,先生。

A : Would you have Dr. Johnson paged, please?
　　請廣播呼叫強森大夫好嗎?

B : Of course.
　　好的。

A : Do you have a paging service?
　　你們有廣播尋人服務嗎?

B : Yes, we do.
　　是的,我們有。

A： I'd like to have someone paged.
　　我想要廣播找一個人。

B： May I have the name, please?
　　請問他叫什麼名字？

A： I'm John Smith. I was just paged. Who wants me?
　　我是約翰・史密斯。剛才有人廣播找我，請問是哪位？

B： There is a phone call for you on line two.
　　二線有您的電話。

《 背景說明 》

　　在大的公司、醫院或公共場所等範圍較廣的地方，找人並不容易，因此必須靠廣播。如果要請播音員廣播找人，就說：*Could you page ~, please?* 然後播音員就會廣播：*Paging ~.* Please come to ~. 或 *Paging ~.* Please meet your party at ~.

【註釋】

page〔pedʒ〕*vt.*（在旅館等）叫侍者去叫（人）；（侍者）喊名找（某人）；廣播找（某人）

May I help you? 我能效勞嗎？（店員常說這句話）

You're welcome. 不客氣；哪裡。（除此一說法，對 Thank you. 最普遍而不拘形式的回答有：Sure.；You bet.）

be supposed to 原來是要；應該是（含有「依原來預定應該如何」，或建議別人應該如何之意。）

This is Ken Davis. 在電話中一開始即表明身份說：「我是…」不可說 "I am…"，必須說 "This is…"

step out 離開家（房間、辦公室）；外出

11. Let's go Dutch.

Dialogue 1

A : Well, how was your date with Steve?
那麼，妳和史提夫約會的情形如何？

B : Terrible!
糟透了！

A : What happened?
出了什麼事？

B : He is so cheap!
他真是吝嗇！

A : What did he do?
他怎麼了？

B : He asked me to go Dutch!
他要我自己付帳。

Dialogue 2

A : This is a charming restaurant.
這是一家迷人的餐館。

B : Yes, it's lovely and the food was delicious.
是啊，它很美，食物也可口。

A : Would you like some more coffee?
你想再來一點咖啡嗎？

B : No, thank you. 不，謝謝。

A : Waiter, may I have the check?
服務生，買單。

B : Tom, let's go Dutch on this.
湯姆，讓我們各付各的吧。

Dialogue 3

A : Jane, I'd like to take you out, but....
　　珍，我想帶妳出去，不過…

B : But what?
　　不過怎麼樣？

A : But it would have to be Dutch treat.
　　不過我們要各付各的。

B : That's fine with me.
　　那好啊。

A : Really?
　　眞的？

B : Sure, where are we going?
　　眞的啊，我們要上哪兒去？

〔舉一反三〕

A : Waiter, I'll take the check.
　　服務生，我要付帳。

B : No, John. Let's go Dutch.
　　不，約翰。我們各付各的。

A : I'd like to take you out to dinner.
　　我想帶你出去吃晚飯。

B : I'd love to go, but I insist we go Dutch.
　　我也想去，不過我堅持各付各的。

A : These theater tickets are expensive.
　　這些戲票眞貴。

B : They sure are. Let's go Dutch.
　　說的也是。讓我們各付各的吧。

A : I like to have dates with Jane.

我喜歡和珍約會。

B : So do I. She likes to go Dutch.

我也是。她喜歡各自付帳。

A : I'll buy my own ticket to the movie.

我自己買我自己的電影票。

B : No, you won't. I'll treat you.

不，你不必了。我請客。

《背景説明》

Go Dutch. 的意思是 Each person pays his own way at a restaurant, movie, etc. 就是中文的「各付各的帳」。這種情形在美國比較普遍，但是在我國，常常是雙方搶著付錢，很少人好意思説「各付各的」，這是民族性的差異。這種搶著付錢的習俗並不是都值得鼓勵，只能説適可而止，以免打腫臉充胖子。因此，學會説：*Let's go Dutch.* 是必要的。當然，能力所及且交情夠的時候，説：*Lunch (or Dinner) is on me.*「午餐（晚餐）我請客。」或 *I'll treat you.*「我請你。」也是一種禮貌。

【註釋】

terrible〔'tɛrəbḷ〕*adv.* 過分地；可怕地；極端地

cheap〔tʃip〕*adj.* 便宜的；吝嗇的　　*go Dutch* 各付各的帳

charming〔'tʃɑrmɪŋ〕*adj.* 迷人的

delicious〔dɪ'lɪʃəs〕*adj.* 好吃的；美味的

check〔tʃɛk〕*n.* 飯館的帳單

take out （口語）帶（女人）結伴出遊

Dutch treat 各自付費的聚餐；費用自備的聚會

date〔det〕*n.* （與異性的）約會　　treat〔trit〕*vt.* 款待；宴饗（某人）

12. He's gone out of business.

Dialogue 1

A : What happened to Joe's gas station?
喬的加油站怎麼了？

B : He's gone out of business.
他已經停止營業了。

A : Why is that?
怎麼會呢？

B : Everybody in Buffalo is going to Canada to fill up his tank.
布法羅的每一個人都到加拿大去裝滿他的油箱。

A : That's too bad. What about your station?
那真不幸。你的加油站如何呢？

B : It's the same for me. I'll have to go out of business before too long.
也是一樣啊。我不久也必須停業。

Dialogue 2

A : That's a good-looking suit.
那套衣服真是漂亮。

B : Thanks, I got it at a good price, too.
謝謝，不過我也是以便宜價錢買得這套衣服。

A : Oh? Where?
哦？在哪兒買的？

B : That men's shop in the mall.
購物中心的男仕專賣店。

A : Do they have other things on sale?
　　他們還有其他東西在減價嗎？

B : Everything's on sale. They're going out of business.
　　每樣東西都在減價。他們快要停業了。

Dialogue 3

A : Joe got a pink slip today.
　　喬今天接到解僱通知。

B : Wow! That's too bad.
　　哇！那太不幸了。

A : And I hear they're going to let other people go
　　next week.
　　而且我又聽說他們下個星期還要解僱其他人。

B : Is business that bad?
　　生意那麼糟嗎？

A : We'll be lucky if this place doesn't fold.
　　如果不關門，我們就算走運了。

B : I'd better start looking for another job.
　　我最好開始另外找工作。

〔舉一反三〕

A : You'd better call Smith's Repair Shop.
　　你最好打電話給史密斯修理廠。

B : I can't, they've gone out of business.
　　不用了。他們已經停業了。

A : My brother's out of work now.
　　我弟弟現在失業了。

B : Did his company go out of business?
　　他的公司關門了嗎？

A : Why are you putting up signs?
你為什麼要張貼告示呢？

B : We're having a going-out-of-business sale.
我們要舉辦歇業大拍賣。

A : How's business lately?
最近生意如何？

B : Bad. I might have to close down permanently.
不好。我可能要永久歇業了。

A : How is your business doing?
你的生意做得怎麼樣了？

B : Badly. It might fold soon.
糟透了。可能很快就會關門。

【註釋】

gas station （汽車的）加油站（供應汽油、機油、水等）（= *service station* ）

go out of business 停業；沒有生意可做　　*fill up* 裝滿；填滿

tank〔tæŋk〕*n.* （水、油、瓦斯等的）桶

before long 不久

good-looking〔'gʊd'lʊkɪŋ〕*adj.* （衣服等）漂亮的；（人）美貌的

suit〔sjut〕*n.* 三件一套的男子服裝（ coat, vest, trousers ）；一套女裝
（ coat, skirt，有時亦包括 blouse ）

mall〔mɔl, mæl〕*n.*（有冷暖氣設備的）購物中心；行人專用的商店街

on sale 廉售；大減價　　*pink slip* 解僱通知

wow〔waʊ〕*int.* 噢；哇（表驚愕、愉快、痛苦等之感歎詞）

let go 革職；撤職　　fold〔fold〕*vi.* 關門大吉

repair shop 修理廠

out of work 失業中；（機器等）發生毛病、故障

put up 張貼（廣告）　　*close down* 歇業；停工；停止做生意

13. It isn't much.

Dialogue 1

A : Mrs. Jones, thank you for your hospitality to me and to my family.

瓊斯太太，謝謝妳對我們一家人的慇勤招待。

B : You're welcome, Mr. Yi.

易先生，你太客氣了。

A : We have a small gift for you.

我們有一樣小禮物要給妳。

B : Oh, thank you, but it isn't necessary to do that.

噢，真是謝謝你了，不過實在不必要這麼做。

A : It isn't much, but we hope you like it.

那是微不足道的，不過希望妳還喜歡它。

B : Oh, I do. Thank you.

噢，我當然喜歡了。謝謝。

Dialogue 2

A : Hi, girls. What are you doing?

嗨，女孩們。妳們在幹什麼？

B : We're selling raffle tickets.

我們正在賣彩票。

A : What's the prize? 獎品是什麼呢？

B : A trip to Miami. 到邁阿密旅行。

A : How much are the tickets?

這些票要多少錢？

B : Not much, just $2.00 each.

不多，每張只售二元。

Dialogue 3

A : Whose dog is that?
　　那隻是誰的狗？

B : Mine, why?
　　我的，怎麼樣？

A : He sure barks a lot.
　　牠的確很會叫。

B : I know. He's really loud.
　　我知道。牠叫得真是大聲。

A : He's not very attractive, either.
　　牠也不太吸引人。

B : He doesn't look like much, but he's a good watchdog.
　　牠看起來並不怎樣，不過是隻好看門狗。

〔舉一反三〕

A : This gift isn't much, but I hope you like it.
　　這件禮物微不足道，不過希望你還喜歡。

B : Thank you. It's lovely.
　　謝謝。這真可愛。

A : Can you lend me $50?
　　你能借我五十元嗎？

B : How about $10? It isn't much, but it's all I can spare.
　　十元如何？雖然不多，不過卻是我所能挪出的全部。

A : Her boyfriend is really ugly.
　　她的男朋友真醜。

B : I know. He's really not much to look at.
　　我知道。他真是不值得一看。

A : How much does that coat cost?

　　那件外套值多少錢？

B : It isn't much, just $100.

　　不多，一百元而已。

A : This room is over-decorated.

　　這房間裝飾得過分了。

B : Yes, it's a bit much, isn't it?

　　對，是有點過頭了，不是嗎？

【註釋】

hospitality〔͵hɑspɪ'tælətɪ〕*n.* 慇勤招待；好客

much〔mʌtʃ〕*adj.* 非常好的；多的；大量的

raffle ticket 彩票

bark〔bɑrk〕*vi.* (指狗、狐狸等) 叫；吠；吼叫

attractive〔ə'træktɪv〕*adj.* 有吸引力的

watchdog〔'wɑtʃ͵dɔg〕*n.* 看門狗

spare〔spɛr〕*vt.* 挪出；騰出

14. Neck and neck.

Dialogue 1

A : What do you think of Ronald Reagan as the Republican candidate for president?
你認爲羅納德・雷根當選共和黨總統候選人如何？

B : I'm disappointed. I supported George Bush.
我有點失望。我支持喬治・布希。

A : A few months ago they were neck and neck in the race. 幾個月前他們在競爭中仍是不分勝負。

B : Now, Bush is second on the ticket.
現在，布希在得票上居第二位。

A : Reagan finally made it. 雷根終於成功了。

B : We'll have to wait and see.
我們仍然要觀望。

Dialogue 2

A : Who's going to get the promotion in our department?
在我們這一部門裏有誰會獲得升遷？

B : I think Bill Jones will get it.
我認爲比爾・瓊斯會升級。

A : What about Tom Anderson?
那你以爲湯姆・安德森如何？

B : Tom is no longer in the running.
湯姆已不再有勝算。

A : Last week everyone said they were neck and neck.
上個星期每個人都說他們兩個不分軒輊。

B : That was last week. Things have changed.
那是上個星期的事。事情已經有了轉變。

Dialogue 3

A : Congratulations, John.
恭喜你啊，約翰。

B : Thanks. 謝謝。

A : You did a great job on your campaign. You deserved to win.
這次競選你幹得很好。你是應該贏的。

B : Thanks, but it was really neck and neck between Tom and me for a while.
謝謝，不過有一陣子湯姆和我實在是不分上下。

A : Tom's a good man, but you're better qualified for this job.
湯姆是個好人，不過你更能勝任這件工作。

B : Thanks. 謝謝。

〔舉一反三〕

A : Was the race close?
這場比賽是不是勝負難分呢？

B : Sure was. It was neck and neck.
是啊。簡直是勢均力敵嘛。

A : It was an exciting game.
這真是場刺激的比賽。

B : The two teams were neck and neck until the last inning. 直到最後一局這兩隊仍是不分勝負。

A : I thought Kennedy would win by a landslide.
我以為甘迺迪會獲得壓倒性的勝利。

B : So did I, but it was really close at the end.
我也是，不過最後結束時仍是相當難分勝負。

A : What color are you going to paint your bedroom?
　　你要在你的臥房漆上什麼顏色？
B : I've narrowed it down to blue or yellow.
　　我已經把顏色減少爲藍色或黃色。

A : My horse barely managed to win that race!
　　我的馬差點贏不了那場比賽！
B : I know! It was almost a dead heat.
　　我知道！那場比賽差點就分不出勝負。

【註釋】

Republican〔rɪ'pʌblɪkən〕adj.（美國）共和黨的
candidate〔'kændə،det,'kændədɪt〕n. 候選人
president〔'prɛzədənt〕n. 總統
disappointed〔،dɪsə'pɔɪntɪd〕adj. 失望的；沮喪的
support〔sə'port,sə'pɔrt〕vt. 支持；擁護
neck and neck（賽跑時）不分上下；並駕齊驅
make it（口語）達成；成功　　promotion〔prə'moʃən〕n. 升遷
department〔dɪ'pɑrtmənt〕n. 部門
What about ~ ?　~ 怎樣？~ 如何？
no longer 不再　　**in the running** 有獲勝的機會；有勝算
congratulation〔kən،grætʃə'leʃən〕n. 祝賀；慶賀；（pl.）祝賀詞
do a great job 把一件事情做得很好
campaign〔kæm'pen〕n. 活動
deserve〔dɪ'zɝv〕vt. 應得；應受（賞罰等）
for a while 一時；暫時　　**be qualified for ~** 勝任；有資格
inning〔'ɪnɪŋ〕n.（棒球）一局
landslide〔'lænd،slaɪd〕n.（選舉的）壓倒性的勝利；山崩
narrow down 縮小範圍　　barely〔'bɛrlɪ〕adv. 幾乎不能
manage〔'mænɪdʒ〕vt. 達成 ~；設法做 ~
dead heat（比賽時兩者以上成績相同）無勝負；平手；並列名次

15. He's in conference now.

Dialogue 1

A : Hello, may I speak to Mr. Yi, please?
哈囉，請易先生聽電話好嗎？

B : I'm sorry, he's in conference now. May I ask who's calling?
對不起，他現在正在開會。請問您貴姓大名？

A : This is Bill Jones. 我是比爾・瓊斯。

B : May I take a message, Mr. Jones?
瓊斯先生，要我留話嗎？

A : Please ask him to call me later this afternoon. He has my number.
請他在今天下午稍後打電話給我。他有我的電話號碼。

B : Yes, sir. Thank you. 好的。謝謝。

Dialogue 2

A : Hello, I'm Bob Robinson. May I speak to the manager, please?
哈囉，我是鮑伯・羅賓森。請經理接電話好嗎？

B : I'm sorry, he's in a meeting now. May I help you with something?
抱歉，他現在正在開會。有什麼事需要我代勞嗎？

A : Perhaps you could. I need some information on your new products for the advertising program.
也許你能。我需要一些你們新產品的資料來做廣告計畫。

B : I can give you some information, but you really should speak to Mr. Green.
我能給你一些資料，不過你真的應該和格林先生談一下。

A : Could I make an appointment for this afternoon?
今天下午我可以約他見面嗎？

B : Yes. He's free at three o'clock.
可以，他三點有空。

Dialogue 3

A : May I help you, sir? 先生，有什麼事嗎？

B : My name is Hanson. I'd like to see Mr. Smith.
我是漢森。我想見史密斯先生。

A : Mr. Smith is with someone else right now. Could you wait? 史密斯先生現在正跟別人在一起。你能等一下嗎？

B : Yes. Do you think he'll be long?
好的。你想他會耗很久嗎？

A : No. He should be free in just a few minutes.
不會的。他應該再過幾分鐘就有空了。

B : Thank you. 謝謝。

〔舉一反三〕

A : I'd like to speak with Mr. Smith.
我想跟史密斯先生講話。

B : I'm sorry, he's in conference now.
抱歉，他現在正在開會。

A : May I see Mr. Green? 我可以見格林先生嗎？

B : I'm sorry, he's in a meeting now.
對不起，他正在開會。

A : May I speak to Mr. Chen?
請陳先生聽電話好嗎？

B : He's not available. May I take a message?
他現在不方便。你要留話嗎？

A ： Is Mr. Jones in？瓊斯先生在嗎？

B ： Yes, but he's with someone else now.
是的，不過他現在正跟別人在一起。

A ： May I speak to Mr. Bok？
請波克生生聽電話好嗎？

B ： He's tied up now. Would you like to leave a message?
他現在正忙著。你要留話嗎？

《背景説明》

在今日繁忙的社會中，開會佔了很重要的角色。甚至有些人天天都有大大小小的會要開，要找到他們並不容易。因此，學會説： **He's in conference now.**「他正在開會。」這句話，常常能派上用場。

如果要説明跟誰在開會，可加上 with ～，例如： He's in conference with a buyer. 或 He's in conference with his staff.

萬一不知道被找的人去了哪裡，可説： **He's not in.** 或 **He's not available.** 很忙不便説明在做什麼時，則用 He's tied up now. 當然 He's in conference now. 也可用 He's in **a meeting** now. 代替，表示相同的意思。

【註釋】

conference〔'kɑnfərəns〕*n.* 會議　　*in conference* 正在舉行會議
manager〔'mænɪdʒɚ〕*n.* 經理
information〔͵ɪnfɚ'meʃən〕*n.* 消息；情報；資訊
product〔'prɑdəkt〕*n.* 產品；產物
advertising〔'ædvɚ͵taɪzɪŋ〕*adj.* 廣告的；有關廣告的
appointment〔ə'pɔɪntmənt〕*n.* 約會
available〔ə'veləbḷ〕*adj.* 可獲得的；有空的
tie up 拘束；使動彈不得，在此引申爲「忙碌」
be tied up in conference 忙於會議（而無空閒）

16. I'm feeling under the weather.

Dialogue 1

A : Hello, Margie？ 喂，瑪琦嗎？

B : Yes. Is this Tom？
   是的。請問是湯姆嗎？

A : Yes. Sorry, Margie, but I'm going to have to break our date.
   是啊。抱歉，瑪琦，我將得取消我們的約會。

B : Why, what's the matter？
   爲什麼，出了什麼事？

A : I'm feeling a little under the weather.
   我覺得身體不大舒服。

B : O.K., maybe we can meet next week.
   好的，也許我們下個星期能見面。

Dialogue 2

A : Isn't Bill here today？ 今天比爾沒到嗎？

B : No, he called in sick.
   是的，他打電話來說他生病。

A : Again？ That's the third time this week.
   又生病了？那已經是這個星期第三次了。

B : He's really been feeling under the weather.
   他實在覺得不舒服。

A : Maybe he needs to see a doctor.
   也許他需要看醫生。

B : Oh, I think he just has a bad cold.
   噢，我認爲他只是得了重感冒罷了。

Dialogue 3

A : That was a disappointment!
真叫人失望！

B : Tom should have won that race.
湯姆應該可以贏得那場比賽。

A : Yeah, I thought he was a cinch.
是啊，我以為他可以穩贏的。

B : I wonder what happened.
我想知道發生了什麼事情。

A : Maybe he doesn't feel well.
也許他覺得不舒服。

B : Yeah, it's hard to run when you're feeling under the weather.
是啊，當你不舒服的時候是很難跑得動。

〔舉一反三〕

A : You look pale.
你看起來臉色蒼白。

B : I'm a little under the weather.
我有點不舒服。

A : Is John here today?
今天約翰到了嗎？

B : No, he's been feeling under the weather.
沒有，他覺得不舒服。

A : Are you feeling under the weather?
你覺得不舒服嗎？

B : Yes, cancel my appointments. I'm going home.
是的，取消我的約會。我要回家了。

A ： I'm feeling under the weather today.
　　我今天不舒服。

B ： Why don't you go home and rest?
　　那你爲什麼不回家休息？

A ： Are you sick?
　　你生病了嗎？

B ： No, just a little under the weather.
　　不是，只是有點不舒服。

〰〰〰〰〰〰〰〰〰〰〰〰〰〰〰〰〰〰〰〰

【註釋】

　break the date 取消約會
　under the weather 生病的；身體不適的
　call in sick 打電話說生病了
　have a bad cold 患了重感冒
　disappointment 〔͵dɪsəˊpɔɪntmənt〕 n. 失望；挫折
　cinch 〔sɪntʃ〕 n. 不負期望的事或人
　pale 〔pel〕 adj. 蒼白的

17. Don't get me wrong.

Dialogue 1

A : Did you hear about the rioters in the Cuban refugee camp?
你聽說古巴難民營裏的暴徒了嗎？

B : Yes, I think we should send them back to Cuba.
是的，我認爲我們應該把他們遣送回古巴。

A : Don't you feel sorry for them?
你不替他們感到難過嗎？

B : Don't get me wrong. I believe in helping refugees, but not rioters.
別誤會我。我堅信要救助難民，但不是要暴徒。

A : I guess many people agree with you.
我猜想很多人會同意你。

B : Yes, President Reagan is one of them.
是的，雷根總統就是其中之一。

Dialogue 2

A : You look tired, Tom.
你看起來很疲倦，湯姆。

B : I am tired. I had a rough day at work.
我是很累了。我工作辛苦了一天。

A : Why don't you quit your job?
爲什麼你不辭去你的工作呢？

B : Oh, I don't want to do that.
噢，我不想那樣做。

A : Why not? You're always tired whenever I see you.
為什麼不想呢？每次我看到你，你總是很疲倦。

B : Don't get me wrong. I like my job.
別誤會我。我喜歡我的工作。

Dialogue 3

A : Bill is going to sing tonight.
比爾今天晚上要唱歌。

B : Oh, no!
噢，不！

A : Don't you like his singing?
你不喜歡他唱歌嗎？

B : It's not that. Don't get me wrong.
不是那樣啦。別誤會我。

A : What's the problem then?
那麼是什麼問題呢？

B : He only knows one song!
他只會一首歌！

〔舉一反三〕

A : I guess you don't like Bob very much.
我想你不很喜歡鮑伯。

B : Don't get me wrong. He's a nice guy but he's lazy.
別誤會我。他是個好人，只不過有點懶。

A : Are you saying he drinks too much?
你是說他喝太多了嗎？

B : Now, don't get me wrong. I just said he liked to drink.
別誤會我了。我只是說他喜歡喝酒。

A : Are you saying she's ugly? 你說她很醜嗎？

B : Don't get me wrong. I just said that I've seen prettier girls.

別誤會我。我只是說我看過更漂亮的女孩子。

A : Are you saying he's a cheapskate?

你是說他是吝嗇鬼？

B : Don't get me wrong. I just meant to say that he is very thrifty. 別誤會我。我的意思是說他很節儉。

A : I resent your criticism.

我厭惡你的批評。

B : Don't misunderstand me. I just want to help you.

別誤會我。我只是想幫你忙。

《背景説明》

　　Don't get me wrong. 中的 get 是 understand 的意思，與 Did you ***get*** it?「你懂了嗎？」中的 get 用法相同。因此，***get sb. wrong*** 就是「誤解某人」。

　　Don't ***misunderstand*** me. 意思與 Don't get me wrong. 相同，只是沒有那麼口語化。

【註釋】

rioter〔'raɪətɚ〕n. 暴徒　　Cuban〔'kjubən〕adj. 古巴的
refugee〔ˌrɛfju'dʒi〕n. 難民　　camp〔kæmp〕n. 營
get sb. wrong 誤解某人的意思　　rough〔rʌf〕adj. 艱苦的
quit〔kwɪt〕vt. 辭職；停止；放棄
now〔naʊ〕adv. 表示轉變話題、解釋等時用
cheapskate〔'tʃip,sket〕n. 吝嗇鬼　　resent〔rɪ'zɛnt〕vt. 憎恨
criticism〔'krɪtɪ,sɪzəm〕n. 批評　　misunderstand〔'mɪsʌndɚ'stænd〕vt. 誤會

18. How late are you open?

Dialogue 1

A : May I help you, sir?
先生，有何貴幹？

B : Yes. How late are you open?
是的。你們營業到幾點？

A : We're open till six on weekdays and till five on weekends.
星期一至五我們營業到六點，週末到五點。

B : Will you be open this Monday?
這星期一你們會開門嗎？

A : No, we won't. That's a holiday and we'll be closed.
不，我們不會。那天是假日，我們關門。

B : Thank you. 謝謝。

Dialogue 2

A : What are you looking for?
你在找什麼？

B : I'm out of cigarettes.
我沒香煙了。

A : There's a shop in the lobby.
在大廳裏有一家商店。

B : I wonder if they're still open.
我想知道他們是不是還開著。

A : Call the front desk and ask.
打電話到櫃台問問看。

B : Good idea. 好主意。

Dialogue 3

A : Why are we stopping?
　　我們爲什麼要停下來?

B : We're out of gas.
　　我們沒有汽油了。

A : Great! Now what?
　　哎呀!現在怎麼辦呢?

B : No problem. There's a station around the corner.
　　沒問題。轉角有個加油站。

A : It's late. I'll bet they're closed.
　　來不及了。我敢說他們已經關門了。

B : No, they're open twenty-four hours a day.
　　不,他們是二十四小時全天營業。

〔舉一反三〕

A : Miss, how late are you open tonight?
　　小姐,今天晚上你們營業到幾點?

B : We're open until nine every night.
　　我們每晚都開到九點。

A : What hours are you open on Sunday?
　　星期日你們營業時間是什麼時候?

B : From ten to five.
　　從十點到五點。

A : What time do you open in the morning?
　　早上你們幾點開門?

B : We open at nine thirty.
　　我們九點半開門。

A : Do you close at six tonight?
今天晚上你們六點關門嗎？

B : No, sir. We're open until ten tonight.
不，先生。今晚我們開到十點。

A : Will you be open tomorrow?
你們明天會開門嗎？

B : No, it's a national holiday. We'll be closed all day.
不，明天是國定假日。我們會全天休業。

【註釋】

open〔'opən〕*adj.*（商店、醫院、學校）開著的；營業的；（戲院）開演中的
vt. 開門；開業；開始

weekdays〔'wik,dez〕*adv.* 每天地（尤指星期一至星期五）

cigarette〔,sɪgə'rɛt〕*n.* 香煙

lobby〔'lɑbɪ〕*n.* 旅館（戲院等）的大廳（休息室）

front desk 櫃台

Great! 哎呀！啊呀！

19. *I'm under a lot of pressure.*

Dialogue 1

A : I'm under a lot of pressure at work.
　　我在工作時受到很大的壓力。

B : How come?
　　怎麼會呢？

A : There's just too much work for one person.
　　這些工作給一個人來做太多了。

B : Maybe you need an assistant.
　　也許你需要一位助手。

A : I'd like one. I never complete one assignment
　　before another one comes along.
　　我是想要一位。我在著手另一件工作之前，從未完成原先的工作。

B : Well, I hope the pressure is off you soon.
　　那麼，我祝你能早點解除這壓力。

Dialogue 2

A : Joanne has been under pressure recently.
　　喬安最近受到壓力。

B : Why's that? 爲什麼？

A : She has to meet a deadline.
　　她必須趕上截止時限。

B : When is the deadline?
　　到何時截止呢？

A : Next Monday. 下星期一。

B : I hope she finishes her work before then.
　　希望她能在那時以前完成她的工作。

Dialogue 3

A : What's wrong with Mary?
瑪麗怎麼了？

B : Oh, she's a nervous wreck.
噢，她精神崩潰了。

A : Why? 為什麼？

B : It's her family. They're really pressuring her to get married.
都是她的家人。他們真的要逼她結婚。

A : I thought she was a dedicated career woman.
我以為她是一個獻身於事業的女人。

B : That's the trouble, she is. But her family doesn't understand her ambition.
那就是麻煩所在，她的確是那種女人。不過她的家人卻不了解她的雄心。

〔舉一反三〕

A : Reagan looks much older now than when he took office. 雷根現在比他剛接任時看起來要老得多了。

B : He's under a lot of pressure.
他受到很大的壓力。

A : Bob seems to be under pressure.
鮑伯似乎受到了壓力。

B : That's because he's got a deadline to meet.
那是因為他要趕上期限。

A : High school students study very hard.
中學生很努力地在讀書。

B : Yes, they're under a lot of pressure to succeed.
是的，他們要成功的壓力很重。

A : Is the boss putting pressure on you?
老闆是否對你施加壓力？

B : Yes, he wants me to increase sales.
是的，他要我增加銷售量。

A : I'm up to my neck in work.
我的工作多得叫我忙不過來。

B : Maybe you need some help.
也許你需要些幫忙。

【註釋】

    pressure (ˈprɛʃɚ) *n.* 壓力；壓迫　　***under pressure*** 受壓迫
    How come? 為什麼？
    assistant (əˈsɪstənt) *n.* 助手　　complete (kəmˈplit) *vt.* 完成
    assignment (əˈsaɪnmənt) *n.* 指派的工作；作業
    recently (ˈrisṇtlɪ) *adj.* 最近；近來
    deadline (ˈdɛd,laɪn) *n.* 截止期限　　***nervous wreck*** 精神崩潰
    dedicated (ˈdɛdə,ketɪd) *adj.* 專注的；虔誠的
    career (kəˈrɪr) *n.* 事業
    ambition (æmˈbɪʃən) *n.* 雄心；野心；抱負
    take office 接任
    sales (selz) *n. pl.* 銷售量
    up to one's neck 被壓倒；幾乎被淹沒於～

20. Five more hours to go.

Dialogue 1

A : Stewardess, may I ask you a question?
空中小姐，可以問妳一個問題嗎？

B : Certainly. What do you want to know?
當然可以。你想知道些什麼？

A : How many more hours until we land in Taipei?
我們還要幾個小時才能在台北著陸？

B : Oh, we have about five more hours to go.
噢，我們大概還得飛五個小時。

A : Thank you, and may I have some coffee?
謝謝，我能要點咖啡嗎？

B : Certainly, and we'll serve dinner in another hour.
當然可以，我們再過一小時會供應晚餐。

Dialogue 2

A : Hi, John. What are you reading?
嗨，約翰。你在看什麼？

B : War and Peace. 「戰爭與和平」。

A : That's a really long book.
那本書真長。

B : Yes, but I'm almost finished with it.
是啊，不過我快看完了。

A : How much more do you have to read?
你還得看多少？

B : Oh, I've only got ten more pages to go.
噢，我還剩十頁。

Dialogue 3

A : I can see the top of the mountain.
我能看到山頂了。

B : Good. How much farther is it?
好極了。還有多遠？

A : About two miles or so.
大約兩哩左右。

B : Well, eight down and two to go.
嗯，我們已經走了八哩，還有兩哩路要走。

A : Think we will make it?
你認爲我們辦得到嗎？

B : Can't turn back now.
現在已經不能折回了。

〔舉一反三〕

A : Haven't you finished that book yet?
你看完了那本書沒有？

B : Almost. I've only got three more pages to go.
差不多。我還剩三頁了。

A : The race is almost over.
比賽快結束了。

B : Yeah, only one more lap to go.
是啊，只剩一圈了。

A : Are we almost home?
我們快到家了嗎？

B : Yes, only one more mile to go.
是的，只剩一哩了。

A : When will you graduate?
　　你何時畢業？

B : Next June. Just one more year to go.
　　明年的六月。只剩一年了。

A : John, turn in your test paper now.
　　約翰，現在交你的考卷。

B : In a minute. I only have two more problems to do.
　　再等一分鐘。我只剩兩題。

【註釋】

stewardess〔'stjuwədɪs〕*n.*（客機、輪船、火車等的）女性服務員；空中小姐
serve〔sɜv〕*vt.* 供應；侍候（顧客）
farther〔'fɑrðə〕*adv.* 更遠的；較遠的（far 的比較級）
lap〔læp〕*n.*（跑道、水道）一周（圈）
graduate〔'grædʒu,et〕*vi.* 畢業

21. I feel the same way.

Dialogue 1

A : This weather is too hot.
天氣太熱了。

B : It sure is.
的確是啊。

A : I can't work. I just want to go to sleep.
我無法工作。我只想睡覺。

B : I feel the same way, but we have to work.
我也有同感，不過我們還是得工作。

A : I guess I'll go buy a coke.
我想去買瓶可口可樂。

B : Pick one up for me, will you?
順便替我買一瓶，好嗎？

Dialogue 2

A : How much time do I have?
我有多少時間？

B : You have to go on stage in five minutes.
再過五分鐘你就得登台了。

A : I'm frightened. 我害怕。

B : Don't worry. You'll do well.
別擔心。你會做得很好。

A : I'm really nervous.
我真的很緊張。

B : I felt the same way the first time I sang on stage.
當我第一次在舞台上唱歌時也有同感。

Dialogue 3

A : How about taking a break?
　　休息一下如何？

B : O.K., I'm tired.
　　好啊，我也累了。

A : I know how you feel. This has been a long day.
　　我了解你的感受。這真是漫長的一天。

B : And it's not over yet.
　　卻還沒過完呢。

A : True. There's still a lot to do.
　　一點也沒錯。還有很多事情要做。

B : We'll be here until midnight.
　　我們要一直待到午夜。

〔舉一反三〕

A : I want to quit my job.
　　我想要辭職。

B : I feel the same way.
　　我有同感。

A : I need a drink.
　　我需要喝一杯。

B : I know how you feel. I'll join you.
　　我知道你的感受。我加入你的行列。

A : All I've done all day is answer the phone.
　　我整天所做的事就是接電話。

B : I feel the same way.
　　我有同感。

A : She talks too much, I think.
　　我覺得她的話太多了。

B : I feel the same way.
　　我有同感。

A : I'm too tired to walk another step.
　　我累得連一步也走不動了。

B : I know how you feel.
　　我了解你的感受。

【註釋】

feel the same way 有同感

coke〔kok〕*n.* （俚語）可口可樂（Coca Cola）

stage〔stedʒ〕*n.* 舞台

frightened〔'fraɪtn̩d〕*adj.* 害怕的

take a break 休息一下

midnight〔'mɪd,naɪt〕*n.* 午夜；半夜

22. *A fifty-fifty chance*.

Dialogue 1

A : I hear Tom Wineglass is running for re-election.
我聽說湯姆‧溫格列斯要競選連任。

B : He'll never win again.
他不會再贏了。

A : Why not?
爲什麼不會呢?

B : He never kept any campaign promises.
他從不遵守競選諾言。

A : Well, I think he has a fifty-fifty chance.
嗯,我認爲他仍然有一半的機會。

B : You want to bet?
你要打賭嗎?

Dialogue 2

A : We're going to vacation at the beach this year.
今年我們要去海濱渡假。

B : Really? When are you going?
眞的?你們什麼時候要去?

A : The last two weeks in April.
四月的最後兩個星期。

B : Aren't you afraid it'll still be cold?
你不擔心天氣仍然會冷嗎?

A : I think we have a fifty-fifty chance for good weather.
我認爲有五成的機會會有好天氣。

B : I wish you luck. 祝你好運。

Dialogue 3

A : What are the chances of our getting tickets to the boxing match?

我們得到拳擊賽入場券的機會有多大呢?

B : Pretty slim. It's going to be a great fight.

很渺茫。這將會是場大比賽。

A : I know. The boxers are really evenly matched.

我知道。拳擊手的實力都是旗鼓相當。

B : I hope Sugar Ray Leonard wins.

我希望蘇格·雷連納德會贏。

A : Well, he's got a 50-50 chance.

嗯,他有五成的機會。

B : True. I just wish I had a ticket.

那倒是真的。不過我只希望能有張票。

〔舉一反三〕

A : Will John win the race?

約翰會贏得這場比賽嗎?

B : I figure he's got a fifty-fifty chance.

我估計他有五成的機會。

A : Will Jim be promoted?

吉姆會升遷嗎?

B : He's got a fifty-fifty chance for it.

他有百分之五十的機會。

A : Will Chris win the prize?

克利斯會贏得獎品嗎?

B : I think he has a 50-50 chance.

我認為他有百分之五十的機會。

A : I'm going to take a chance and bet on him.
　　我要碰碰運氣，在他身上下賭注。
B : You might win. The odds are even.
　　你可能會贏。機會均等。

A : Will Tom win the election?
　　湯姆會贏得選舉嗎？
B : I don't think so. His chances are slim.
　　我不認為如此。他的希望渺茫。

【註釋】

re-election 〔ˌriə'lɛkʃən 〕 n. 再選；再度當選
promise 〔'prɑmɪs 〕 n. 諾言；約定
keep a promise 遵守諾言
a fifty-fifty chance 百分之五十的機會
beach 〔 bitʃ 〕 n. 海濱
boxing match 拳擊賽
slim 〔 slɪm 〕 adj. 微小的；細長的
fight 〔 faɪt 〕 n. 拳擊比賽
boxer 〔'bɑksə 〕 n. 拳擊手
match 〔 mætʃ 〕 vt. 與～匹敵；為～之好對手
The odds are even. 無優劣之差；機會平等。

23. *She stood me up.*

Dialogue 1

A : Why are you home so early, Tom?
湯姆，你爲什麼這麼早就到家了？

B : So early? I didn't go anywhere.
這麼早？我又沒上哪兒去。

A : I thought you had a date with Sally.
我以爲你和莎莉有約會。

B : So did I.
我也是以爲這樣。

A : Well, what happened?
那麼，怎麼了？

B : She stood me up.
她讓我白等了。

Dialogue 2

A : What's the problem, Jerry?
傑瑞，有什麼問題嗎？

B : I had a lousy time last night.
昨晚過得眞差勁。

A : Weren't you going on a date with Linda?
你不是跟琳達約會嗎？

B : I was, but she stood me up.
是啊，不過她讓我空等了。

A : That's terrible. 那眞糟糕。

B : Yeah. I went to her house and she'd already gone out. 是啊，我去她家，而她卻已經出去了。

Dialogue 3

A : What's wrong, Judy?
茱蒂，怎麼了？

B : Everything's wrong!
每件事情都不對勁！

A : What happened?
什麼事？

B : I had a date with Tom tonight and I waited for
two whole hours.
今晚我和湯姆約會，而我足足等了兩個小時。

A : So he was late. Big deal!
他遲到，有什麼了不起！

B : He wasn't just late. He never showed up.
他不僅是遲到。他根本就沒來。

〔舉一反三〕

A : I thought you had a date with Jane.
我以爲你和珍有約會。

B : I did, but she stood me up.
我是和她有約會，不過她卻讓我空等。

A : What time is your date?
你的約會是什麼時候？

B : It was two hours ago. I got stood up.
兩個小時以前。我白等了。

A : Why is Sue at home?
蘇爲什麼在家？

B : Tom stood her up.
湯姆放她鴿子。

A : Why did you stand me up last night?
　　昨晚你為什麼讓我空等？
B : I forgot about our date.
　　我忘了我們的約會。

A : Didn't you have a date with Jim last night?
　　昨晚妳不是和吉姆約會嗎？
B : Yes, but he never showed up.
　　是啊，不過他一直都沒露面。

【註釋】

stand sb. up （俚語）使（人）空等；爽約；放某人鴿子
lousy（'lauzɪ）*adj.*（俚語）討厭的；卑鄙的；差勁的
show up 出現

> I thought you had a date with Sally.

> She stood me up.

24. *Who's in charge?*

Dialogue 1

A : Miss, who's in charge of customer complaints?
小姐，顧客不滿找誰？

B : What's the problem, sir?
先生，有什麼事嗎？

A : I bought this coffee pot here yesterday and it's defective.
昨天我在這兒買了咖啡壺，而它有缺點。

B : Do you have your sales receipt?
你有收據嗎？

A : Yes, right here.
有，在這兒。

B : Take the coffee pot and your receipt to the Customer Service Desk on the second floor and they'll give you a refund.
拿著咖啡壺和你的收據去二樓的顧客服務台，他們會退錢給你。

Dialogue 2

A : What do you do for a living?
你做什麼來謀生？

B : I'm with BCM International.
我在 BCM 國際公司做事。

A : Where is the company located?
公司位於哪裏？

B : In Chicago.
在芝加哥。

A : What do you do there?
你在那裏做什麼？
B : I'm in charge of overseas marketing.
我負責海外市場。

Dialogue 3

A : That salesgirl was rude to a customer.
那個女店員對顧客不禮貌。
B : I know, but she's new here.
我知道，不過她是新來的。

A : Who hired her? 是誰雇用她呢？
B : I think Mrs. Jones did.
我想是瓊斯太太。

A : Why don't you know? 你為什麼不知道呢？
B : I'm not sure who's in charge of hiring.
我不確定誰負責僱人。

〔舉一反三〕

A : Who's in charge of this store?
誰在負責管理這家店？
B : Not me. I just work here.
不是我。我只是在這裏工作。

A : Who's in charge here? 誰負責管理這裏？
B : Mr. Johnson. He's the manager.
強森先生。他是經理。

A : Who's responsible for this department?
誰負責這一部門？
B : Mr. Thompson. He's in charge.
湯普遜先生。是他負責管理的。

A : Who controls the money in your family?
　　　在你家裏是誰掌管金錢？
B : My husband. He's in charge of that.
　　　我先生。是他負責管理的。

A : Who's in charge of the ship?
　　　誰負責管理這艘船？
B : The captain. He's in command.
　　　船長。由他負責統率。

《背景說明》

　　　注意下面兩個片語的差別：*be in charge of* ～「負責管理～」；
be in the charge of ～「由～負責管理」。

　　　詢問「誰負責這裡？」或「誰負責這個部門？」用 *Who's in charge*
here? 或 *Who's in charge of* this department？回答則說：～ *is in*
charge. 或 I don't know.

【註釋】

in charge of 負責管理　　*coffee pot* 咖啡壺
pot〔pɑt〕*n.* 壺；瓶；罐；盆；鍋等容器或烹飪器
defective〔dɪ'fɛktɪv〕*adj.* 有缺點的；不完美的
receipt〔rɪ'sit〕*n.* 收據　　refund〔'ri,fʌnd〕*n.* 退款
be located 位於（= *be situated* ）　　overseas〔'ovɚ'siz〕*adj.* 海外的
marketing〔'mɑrkɪtɪŋ〕*n.* 在市場之交易；買賣；行銷
salesgirl〔'selz,gɝl〕*n.* 女店員；女售貨員
rude〔rud〕*adj.* 無禮的　　hire〔haɪr〕*vt.* 僱；請；租
responsible〔rɪ'spɑnsəb!〕*adj.* 負責任的；有責任的
command〔kə'mænd〕*vt.* 統率；指揮

25. There's a call for you.

Dialogue 1

A : Mr. Jones, there's a call for you.
瓊斯先生，有你的電話。

B : Find out who it is and tell him I'll call back.
問他是誰，並告訴他我會打電話過去。

A : It's your wife.
你太太。

B : Tell her I'll call back later.
告訴她等一下我會打電話回去。

A : She says it's urgent.
她說有要緊的事。

B : I'll take it in my office.
我在辦公室接聽好了。

Dialogue 2

A : Mr. Brown, there's a call for you.
布朗先生，有你的電話。

B : Who is it? 誰啊？

A : Mr. Smith.
史密斯先生。

B : Tell him I'll call him later.
告訴他我待會兒打電話給他。

A : It's the third time he's called today.
這是他今天第三次打電話來。

B : All right, put him through.
好吧，把他的電話接進來好了。

Dialogue 3

A : Were there any calls for me while I was out?
我出去的時候有沒有我的電話？

B : Just one. Mr. Smith called around one o'clock.
只有一通。大約在一點鐘的時候史密斯先生打來過。

A : Mr. Smith?
史密斯先生？

B : Of the Sunkist Company.
香吉士公司的那一位。

A : Oh, did he say what he wanted?
噢，他有沒有說要幹什麼？

B : Yes, you were supposed to meet him at twelve for lunch and he was still waiting.
有的，你應該在十二點和他見面吃午飯，而他卻一直在等。

〔舉一反三〕

A : Mr. Green, there's a call for you.
格林先生，有你的電話。

B : Take a message and I'll call back later.
記一下，待會兒我會打過去。

A : Did anyone call?
有人打電話來嗎？

B : Yes, your wife. She wants you to call her.
有啊，你太太。她要你打電話給她。

A : Mr. Jones, can you take a call on line two?
瓊斯先生，你能接一下二線的電話嗎？

B : Yes.
好的。

A : Mr. Stone, Mr. Lee's on the line.
　　史東先生，李先生打電話來。

B : I'll take it in my office.
　　我在辦公室接。

A : Joe, it's for you.
　　喬，你的電話。

B : I'll use the other phone.
　　我用另外一支電話。

【註釋】

There's a call for you. 有你的電話。

urgent (ˈɝdʒənt) *adj.* 緊急的；迫切的

be supposed to 應該

26. *Will you accept the charge?*

Dialogue 1

A : Hello, I'd like to make a collect call to Taipei, Taiwan.
喂，我要撥一通由受話人付款的電話到台灣台北。

B : What number, please, and to whom do you wish to speak?
請問號碼幾號，還有你想跟誰通話？

A : I'd like to speak to Mr. Lee at 783-2192.
我想跟 783-2192 號的李先生通話。

B : What's your name, sir?
先生，請問您貴姓大名？

A : My name is B-O-K. Bok.
我叫 B-O-K。波克。

B : Hello, Mr. Lee? There's a collect call from Mr. Bok. Will you accept the charge?
喂，李先生嗎？有一通由波克先生打來的電話，你願意支付費用嗎？

Dialogue 2

A : Hi, Mom.
嗨，媽。

B : John, this phone bill is much too high!
約翰，電話費實在太高了！

A : Why? What's wrong?
為什麼？怎麼了？

B : There are too many long distance calls on it.
這上面有太多通長途電話了。

A : But my girlfriend wants me to call her.
可是我的女朋友要我打電話給她。

B : Then ask her to accept the charge and call her collect!
那麼叫她付款，打電話由她自己出錢。

Dialogue 3

A : Have you heard from your son who's living in the United States?
你有沒有在美國的兒子的消息？

B : Yes, he called.
有啊，他打電話來過。

A : It must have been good to hear his voice again.
能再聽見他的聲音一定很愉快。

B : Yes, it was, but I would rather have had a letter.
是啊，不過我倒寧願接封信。

A : Why? 為什麼？

B : He called collect!
他打的是對方付費的電話。

〔舉一反三〕

A : I have a collect call for Mr. Bok from Mr. Cosnow. Will you accept the charge?
我有一通由科斯諾打給波克的對方付費電話。你願意付款嗎？

B : Yes, operator.
好的，接線生。

A : My son has found a way to save money on phone calls. 我兒子發現了省電話費的方法。

B : What does he do, call collect?
他怎麼做呢，要受話人付錢嗎？

A： Will you accept the charge for a collect call from Mr. Lee?

你願意替李先生打來的對方付費電話付錢嗎？

B： No, no one is in the office right now.

不行，現在沒有人在辦公室。

A： Can I make a collect call from a pay phone?

我可以用公共電話打一通由受話人付款的電話嗎？

B： Sure. Just call the operator.

可以啊。只要打給接線生就行了。

A： I'm expecting a call from Mr. Yi from Taipei, Taiwan.

我正在等由台灣台北的易先生打來的電話。

B： Should I accept the charge if he calls collect?

如果他打來的是由受話人付款的電話，我該付錢嗎？

【註釋】

a collect call 一通由受話人付款的電話

accept the charge 認付費用

phone bill 電話費繳交通知單

long distance call 長途電話

would rather 寧願

operator〔ˈɑpəˌretɚ〕*n.* 接線生

pay phone 公共電話

27. What's this regarding?

Dialogue 1

A : Mr. Smith's office.
史密斯先生的辦公室。

B : Hello, this is Tom Jones. May I speak with Mr. Smith?
喂,我是湯姆・瓊斯。我可以和史密斯先生通話嗎?

A : I'm sorry, he's out of the office. May I take a message?
抱歉,他出去了。要我留話嗎?

B : No, but maybe you can help me.
不用了,不過也許你可以幫我的忙。

A : I'll try, sir. What is this regarding?
我試試看,先生。請問是關於哪一方面?

B : My contract with Mr. Hart.
我和哈特先生的契約。

Dialogue 2

A : Any messages for me, Miss Gray?
有人留話給我嗎?蓋瑞小姐。

B : Mr. Brown called while you were out.
你出去的時候布朗先生打電話來。

A : Regarding what?
關於哪一方面?

B : He wanted information about the labor contract.
他要有關於勞工契約的資料。

A : Get him on the phone for me.
　　替我接個電話給他。

B : Yes, sir.
　　好的。

Dialogue 3

A : Hello, Miss Thompson. What's new?
　　哈囉，湯普森小姐。有什麼事？

B : There's a memo on your desk from the head office.
　　在你的桌上有一張來自總公司的便箋。

A : What's it regarding?
　　是關於什麼的？

B : The vacation schedule.
　　假期時間表。

A : Good! Has it been approved?
　　好極了！被核准了嗎？

B : No. All vacations have been cancelled.
　　沒有。所有的假期都被取消了。

〔舉一反三〕

A : I need to speak to Mr. Smith.
　　我必需和史密斯先生說話。

B : What is this regarding, sir?
　　先生，請問是關於哪一方面？

A : John called me yesterday.
　　昨天約翰打電話給我。

B : Regarding what?
　　關於什麼？

A : We need to talk, Bill.
　　比爾，我們需要談一談。

B : Regarding what?
　　關於哪一方面？

A : I sent you a note regarding the contract.
　　我寄給你一張關於契約的通知。

B : I didn't receive it.
　　我沒有收到。

A : May I help you, sir?
　　要我幫你忙嗎，先生？

B : I have a complaint regarding my bill.
　　關於我的帳單，我要提出控訴。

【註釋】

regarding (rɪˈgɑrdɪŋ) *prep.* 關於；至於
contract (ˈkɑntrækt, ˈkɑntrækt) *n.* 合約；合同
labor (ˈlebɚ) *n.* 勞工；勞動
memo (ˈmɛmo) *n.* 備忘錄；便箋；同一機構內之簽條
head office 總公司；總局；總社
schedule (ˈskɛdʒʊl) *n.* 時間表；目錄；一覽表
approve (əˈpruv) *vt.* 贊成；贊許
cancel (ˈkænsl̩) *vt.* 取消；刪去
complaint (kəmˈplent) *n.* 訴苦；抱怨

28. *May I see your boarding pass, please?*

Dialogue 1

A : May I see your boarding pass, please?
我可以看看你的登機證嗎?

B : Here it is. Where is my seat?
在這兒。我的位子在哪裏?

A : 13A is on the right side.
13A 在右邊。

B : Thank you.
謝謝。

A : What would you like to drink?
你想喝些什麼?

B : Orange juice, please.
橘子汁。

Dialogue 2

A : What can I do with this bag, Miss?
小姐,這袋子我該怎麼辦?

B : Please put it under your seat or in the overhead bin.
請放在你的座位下或是頭頂上的箱子裏。

A : Is this O.K.?
這樣就可以了嗎?

B : Yes, that's fine.
對,這就行了。

A : Thank you
　　謝謝。

B : You're welcome.
　　不客氣。

Dialogue 3

A : Would you like a drink before dinner?
　　你想在晚飯前喝一杯嗎？

B : Yes, a martini, please.
　　好啊，請給我一杯馬丁尼酒。

A : Here you are. Which would you prefer for dinner, fish or pork?
　　你要的在這兒。你晚餐比較喜歡吃什麼，魚肉還是豬肉？

B : The pork, please.
　　豬肉。

A : What do you want with your dinner, coffee or tea?
　　你晚餐還要些什麼，咖啡還是茶？

B : Tea, please.
　　茶。

〔舉一反三〕

A : Would you like something to drink?
　　你想喝些什麼嗎？

B : Yes. May I have some coffee?
　　好啊。我可以來點咖啡嗎？

A : What time do we land in Chicago?
　　我們什麼時候在芝加哥著陸？

B : At 3:15, sir.
　　三點十五分，先生。

A : Are you going to serve dinner on this flight?
在這次飛行途中你們供應晚餐嗎？

B : No, sir. Just a snack.
不，先生。只有點心而已。

A : May I have a pillow and blanket?
我可以要枕頭和毯子嗎？

B : Sure. I'll get them for you.
可以啊。我拿給你。

A : May I smoke here?
我可以在這裡抽煙嗎？

B : No, sir. You'll have to go to the smoking section in the rear.
不行。你必須到後面的抽煙區才行。

【註釋】

boarding pass 登機證

juice 〔dʒus〕 *n.* (水果、蔬菜、肉等之) 汁；液

overhead 〔'ovə‚hɛd〕 *adj.* 在頭上的；在上面的

bin 〔bɪn〕 *n.* 貯藏箱；櫃

martini 〔mɑr'tinɪ〕 *n.* 馬丁尼酒

Here you are. 你要的東西在這裏。

pork 〔pork, pɔrk〕 *n.* 豬肉

pillow 〔'pɪlo〕 *n.* 枕頭

blanket 〔'blæŋkɪt〕 *n.* 毛毯

rear 〔rɪr〕 *n.* 後半部；背後

29. What's the purpose of your visit?

Dialogue 1

A : What's your name, please?

請問您貴姓大名？

B : Mei-hua Yi.

易美華。

A : What's the purpose of your visit?

您到這裏有什麼目的？

B : I'm a student. I will be attending the summer program at UCLA.

我是學生。我將參加加州大學洛杉磯分校的暑期課程。

A : How long will you be here?

您會在這兒待多久？

B : For eight weeks.

八週。

Dialogue 2

A : What's your name, sir?

先生，您貴姓大名？

B : Ta-wei Lee.

李大維。

A : What's the purpose of your visit?

您到這裏來的目的是什麼？

B : Business. I'm here to attend a sales meeting in Chicago.

生意。我到這兒參加一項在芝加哥的銷售會議。

A : What company are you with?
　　您是在哪家公司服務？
B : BCM International.
　　BCM 國際公司。

Dialogue 3

A : May I have your name, please?
　　請問您貴姓大名？
B : My name is Yang-hua Kao.
　　我叫高仰華。

A : What's the purpose of your visit?
　　您此行有何目的？
B : I'm here to visit my daughter.
　　我到這兒來探望我女兒。

A : How long are you going to stay?
　　您準備待多久？
B : One month.
　　一個月。

〔舉一反三〕

A : What's the purpose of your visit?
　　您此行有何目的？
B : I'll be studying at the University of Illinois.
　　我準備就讀於伊利諾大學。

A : What is your destination in the United States?
　　您在美國的目的地是哪裏？
B : I plan to travel to New York.
　　我計劃到紐約。

A : When do you plan to return to your home country?
　　你計畫何時回到祖國？

B : In June.
　　六月。

A : How long are you going to stay in this country?
　　你將在這個國家待多久？？

B : For one month.
　　　一個月。

A : How long has your daughter lived in the United States?
　　你女兒在美國住多久了？

B : She's lived here for three years.
　　她已經住三年了。

【註釋】

purpose〔'pɝpəs〕*n.* 目的；意圖

U.C.L.A. University of California (Los Angeles division) 加大
　洛杉磯分校

destination〔ˌdɛstə'neʃən〕*n.* 目的地

30. *Take me to the Hilton Hotel, please.*

Dialogue 1

A : Take me to the Hilton Hotel in Taipei, please.
請帶我到台北的希爾頓飯店。

B : O.K.
好的。

A : How far is it from here?
離這兒有多遠呢？

B : About five miles. It'll take maybe thirty minutes this time of night.
大約五哩。晚上這個時候大約要花三十分鐘。

A : About how much will the fare be?
大概要多少車費？

B : Around NT$ 100.
大約台幣一百元。

Dialogue 2

A : Take me to 4550 West Wilson Avenue, please.
請帶我到威爾森西街 4550 號。

B : All right. (*a little later*) Here we are.
好的。（過了一會兒）我們到了。

A : How much is the fare?
車費多少？

B : $ 8.25.
八塊二毛五。

A : Keep the change. 別找了。

B : Thank you. 謝謝。

Dialogue 3

A : Take me to 1424 Johnson Street.
　　到強生街 1424 號。

B : Is that near the stadium?
　　離體育館很近嗎？

A : Yes, just south of it.
　　是啊，就在它的南邊。

B : O.K. I know the area.
　　好的，我知道那地方。

A : How long will it take?
　　要多久才能到？

B : About twenty minutes.
　　大約二十分鐘。

〔舉一反三〕

A : Take me to the bus station, please.
　　請帶我到巴士站。

B : Which one, Greyhound or Trailways?
　　哪一家的，灰狗巴士還是拖曳巴士？

A : Take me to Dodger Stadium.
　　到道奇運動場。

B : Do you want the main entrance?
　　你要到正門嗎？

A : Take me to 510 North Michigan Avenue.
　　到密西根北街 510 號。

B : Is that the ROC Consulate?
　　那是中華民國的領事館嗎？

A : Can you take me up to the main door?
　　你能帶我到正門嗎？

B : No, I can't drive that close, you'll have to get out here.
　　不行，我無法開那麼近，你得在這兒下車。

A : I have to catch a plane. Can't you hurry?
　　我要搭飛機，你能不能快點？

B : I'm going as fast as I can.
　　我已經儘量開快了。

【註釋】

fare〔fɛr〕*n.* 車資；船費
avenue〔'ævə,nju〕*n.* 大街
change〔tʃendʒ〕*n.* 零錢
Keep the change. 不用找零錢了。
stadium〔'stediəm〕*n.* 運動場；體育館；競技場
area〔'ɛrɪə,'erɪə〕*n.* 地區；地方；區域
entrance〔'ɛntrəns〕*n.* 入口；大門
consulate〔'kɑnslɪt,'kɑnsjəlɪt〕*n.* 領事館

O.K.

Take me to the Hillton Hotel in Taipei, please.

31. Do you have a single room available?

Dialogue 1

A : May I help you?
　　我能幫你的忙嗎？

B : Yes. Do you have a single room available?
　　是的。你們有空的單人房嗎？

A : When are you checking in?
　　您什麼時候要登記遷入呢？

B : Tonight.
　　今晚。

A : For how many nights, sir?
　　先生，您要住幾個晚上？

B : I'd like to stay five nights and check out Saturday morning.
　　我想待五個晚上，然後在星期六早上結帳遷出。

Dialogue 2

A : I'd like a room, please.
　　我想要一間房間。

B : Single or double, sir?
　　單人房還是雙人房？

A : Single, please. Just for one night.
　　單人房。只住一個晚上。

B : All right, sir. Sign here.
　　好的，先生。請在這兒簽字。

A : How late is your restaurant open?

　　你們的餐廳營業到幾點？

B : They serve dinner until nine.

　　他們供應晚餐直到九點為止。

Dialogue 3

A : Do you have a reservation, sir?

　　先生，您預先訂了嗎？

B : Yes, the name is John Smith.

　　是的，名字是約翰‧史密斯。

A : Yes. I have it here. A single room for five nights?

　　是的，我找到了。要單人房住五個晚上，對不對？

B : That's right.

　　對了。

A : Please sign here, sir. The porter will take your bags.

　　請在這兒簽個名，先生。侍者會幫你提袋子的。

B : Thank you.

　　謝謝。

〔舉一反三〕

A : Are you checking in now?

　　你現在就要登記住宿嗎？

B : Yes. Do you have a single room available?

　　是的。你們有沒有空的單人房？

A : I'd like a single room, please.

　　我想要一間單人房。

B : Sorry, sir. We're full.

　　對不起，先生。我們已經客滿了。

A : What is the check-out time?

結帳退房的時間呢？

B : 11 :30, sir.

十一點三十分，先生。

A : I'll be checking out tomorrow morning at eight.

我將在明天早上八點結帳退房。

B : I'll have your bill ready, sir.

先生，我會替你準備好帳單。

A : My room is too close to the elevator. Can I change it?

我的房間太靠近電梯了。我能換個房間嗎？

B : Sorry, sir. Nothing else is vacant.

抱歉，先生。沒別的空房間了。

【註釋】

single〔'sɪŋgl̩〕adj. 單獨的　　*single room* 單人房

available〔ə'veləbl̩〕adj. 可獲得的；可利用的，在本課則表示「空的；現成可以住的」

check in 到達旅館時辦理登記手續

check out 付清帳而離開旅館

vacant〔'vekənt〕adj. 空的

32. Can you give me a wake-up call at six?

Dialogue 1

A : May I help you?
我能幫忙嗎?

B : Yes. Can you give me a wake-up call at six?
是的。你能不能六點打電話叫我起床?

A : Hang on. I'll transfer your call to the front desk.
別掛斷。我替你轉接到櫃台。

B : May I help you?
我能幫忙嗎?

A : Yes. Can you give me a wake-up call at six?
是的。你能不能六點打電話叫我起床?

B : Surely.
好的。

Dialogue 2

A : I know I forgot to pack something!
我想起來我忘了裝一樣東西!

B : What did you forget?
你忘了什麼?

A : My alarm clock.
我的鬧鐘。

B : No problem.
沒問題。

A : No problem? How will we ever wake up on time?
　　沒問題？那我們怎能準時起床呢？

B : Just call the desk and ask for a wake-up call.
　　只要打給櫃台，要他們打電話叫我們起床就行了。

Dialogue 3

A : The tour bus is waiting for you, Mr. Lee.
　　遊覽車正在等你呢，李先生。

B : I'm sorry. I overslept.
　　真抱歉。我睡過頭了。

A : Didn't you get a wake-up call this morning?
　　今天早上你沒要櫃台用電話叫醒你嗎？

B : Yes, I did.
　　有啊。

A : What happened?
　　到底是怎麼了？

B : I went back to sleep.
　　我又睡著了。

〔舉一反三〕

A : This is room 503. Could I have a wake-up call
　　at 7:30?
　　這裡是 503 室。請在七點三十分叫醒我好嗎？

B : Certainly, sir. Room 503, 7:30.
　　好的，先生。503 室，七點三十分。

A : The tour bus leaves at 9:15.
　　遊覽車在九點十五分開。

B : We'd better have a wake-up call at eight.
　　我們最好請櫃台在八點用電話叫醒我們。

A : Who was on the phone?
　　　誰打電話來？
B : That was our wake-up call.
　　　那是來通知我們起床的。

A : I'm in room 706. Can you give me a wake-up call at six?
　　　我在 706 室。請你在六點鐘打電話叫醒我好嗎？
B : Certainly, sir.
　　　好的，先生。

A : Front desk? This is Mr. Lee in room 507. Can you give me a wake-up call at six?
　　　櫃台嗎？我是 507 室的李先生。請在六點打電話叫醒我好嗎？
B : Certainly, sir. Room 507 at six.
　　　好的，先生。507 室，六點。

【註釋】

wake-up call 旅館中的服務，可由櫃台的服務生照您吩咐的時間打電話到房間，提醒您起床。

transfer〔træns'fɝ〕*vt.* 轉移；轉接

pack〔pæk〕*vt.* 裝；包裝；打包

tour bus 遊覽車

oversleep〔'ovɚ'slip〕*vi.* 睡過頭

33. Could you suggest some interesting places to visit?

Dialogue 1

A : Hello, could you help me? I just arrived in Taipei.
哈囉，你能幫我的忙嗎？我剛到台北。

B : I'll try. What do you want?
我試試看。你需要些什麼？

A : Could you suggest some interesting places to visit while I'm here?
你能建議一下，我在這兒時有哪些有趣的地方可以看一看嗎？

B : Yes, you should be sure to visit the Presidential Palace, and the National Palace Museum during your stay in Taiwan.
是的，當你在台灣的時候，應該去看一看總統府，和國立故宮博物院。

A : Thanks a lot. Are these places easy to get to?
多謝了。這些地方很容易就可以到嗎？

B : Sure, they're right here in town. 是啊，就在城裏。

Dialogue 2

A : How much longer will you be in Taipei, Jim?
吉姆，你還要在台北待多久？

B : I have four full days before I have to leave.
在我離開之前還有四天整的時間。

A : Four days? Do you have any plans?
四天？你有任何計畫嗎？

B : No, but I would like to do some sightseeing outside of Taipei. Do you have any suggestions?
沒有，不過我想到台北以外的地方去觀光。你有什麼建議嗎？

A : Well, you could fly down to Orchid Island for a few days or you could spend your time at Mt. Ali. Both places are beautiful.

你可以坐飛機到蘭嶼過幾天或是到阿里山。這兩個地方都很美。

B : I think I'll try the island.

我想我會去蘭嶼試試看。

Dialogue 3

A : Good morning, Miss Chen. 早安，陳小姐。

B : Good morning. Have you and your wife enjoyed your visit to Taipei, Mr. Smith?

早安，史密斯先生。您和您太太還喜歡這次的台北之旅嗎？

A : Oh, very much. I'm just sorry we have to leave tomorrow.

噢，很喜歡。不過真遺憾我們明天就得走了。

B : Do you have any special plans for your last day?

最後一天你們有什麼特別的計畫嗎？

A : I would like to take my wife someplace special for dinner. Can you recommend a good restaurant?

我想帶我太太到一個特別的地方吃晚飯。你能推薦一家好餐館嗎？

B : Oh, yes. There's an excellent Chinese restaurant in the next block.

噢，好的。下一個街區有一家很好的中國餐館。

〔舉一反三〕

A : I'm a tourist here. Can you suggest some interesting places to visit?

我是個觀光客。您能建議一些可以去的好玩地方嗎？

B : Sure. Don't miss the National Palace Museum.

好的。別錯過了國立故宮博物院。

A : I only have a few days in town. Can you suggest some things to do and see while I'm here?

我只能在城裏待幾天而已。趁我還在這裏時,你能建議我該做些什麼和看些什麼嗎?

B : Sure. I'd be glad to help you.

好的。我會樂意幫助你。

A : Who's he? 他是誰?

B : A tour guide. He just suggested some things that we should see. 一個導遊。他剛建議我們一些該看的東西。

A : I'm new in town. Can you recommend a good restaurant?

我是剛到這一城的。你能推薦一家好餐館嗎?

B : Yes. Try the Chinese restaurant on the corner.

好的。你試試在轉角的中國餐館。

A : Which dish do you recommend in this restaurant?

你要推薦這家餐館裡的哪一道菜呢?

B : I suggest you try the ribs. They're great here.

我建議你試試看排骨。這裏的排骨很好吃。

【註釋】

the Presidential Palace 總統府

the National Palace Museum 故宮博物院

museum〔 mju'ziəm , mju'zɪəm 〕 *n.* 博物院;博物館

sightseeing〔'saɪt,siɪŋ〕 *n.* 觀光;遊覽   orchid〔'ɔrkɪd〕 *n.* 蘭花

recommend〔,rɛkə'mɛnd〕 *vt.* 推薦;介紹

excellent〔'ɛkslənt〕 *adj.* 特優的;很棒的

block〔blɑk〕 *n.* 街區(四面臨街的一大片建築物)

tourist〔'turɪst〕 *n.* 遊客;觀光客

tour guide 導遊   dish〔dɪʃ〕 *n.* 菜餚

34. *Can you break a twenty dollar bill?*

Dialogue 1

A : May I help you, sir?
先生，要我幫忙嗎？

B : I want to buy this magazine.
我要買這本雜誌。

A : That'll be seventy-five cents, sir.
七十五分錢，先生。

B : Can you break a twenty dollar bill?
您能把一張二十元的鈔票換開嗎？

A : Sure, if you don't mind getting a lot of singles.
可以啊，只要你不介意拿很多一元的鈔票就行了。

B : That's O.K.
好的。

Dialogue 2

A : Lend me a dollar, will you?
借我一塊錢，好嗎？

B : Why?
為什麼？

A : I have to pay the parking fee and all I have is a twenty.
我得付停車費，而我只有一張二十元的鈔票。

B : Ask them to break it for you.
要他們替你換開啊。

A : They never have change this time of night.
　　晚上的這個時候他們沒有零錢啊。

B : They'd better, because I don't have a dollar.
　　最好他們有，因爲我沒有一塊錢。

Dialogue 3

A : I forgot to buy cigarettes while we were out.
　　我們出去的時候，我忘了買香煙。

B : There's a machine in the lobby.
　　大廳裏有一部機器。

A : Do you have any change？ All I have is a twenty.
　　你有零錢嗎？我只有一張二十元的鈔票。

B : No, I don't.
　　沒有。

A : Maybe the front desk can break it for me.
　　也許櫃台能幫我換開。

B : I'm sure they can.
　　我確信他們能。

〔舉一反三〕

A : The bill is ＄2.50, sir.
　　先生，帳單是兩塊五毛錢。

B : Can you break a twenty dollar bill？
　　你能換開一張二十元的鈔票嗎？

A : Can you break a twenty？
　　你能換開一張二十元的鈔票嗎？

B : No, sir. You must have the exact change to ride the bus.
　　不行，先生。你必須有確實數目的零錢才能搭公車。

A : Will you pay for the popcorn? All I have is a twenty.
　　你付買爆米花的錢好嗎？我只有一張二十元的鈔票。

B : He can give you change.
　　他可以找零錢給你。

A : Can you change a twenty? I need some quarters.
　　您能兌換一張二十元的鈔票嗎？我需要一些二角五分的硬幣。

B : Sure. How many quarters do you need?
　　好的。您需要幾個二角五分的硬幣？

A : Can I pay you later? All I have is a twenty.
　　我可以等一下再付錢給你嗎？我只有一張二十元的鈔票。

B : I can break it for you.
　　我可以替你換開。

【註釋】

magazine〔͵mæɡəˈzin,ˈmæɡə͵zin〕n. 雜誌
break〔brek〕vt. 兌換～成零錢；換開
single〔ˈsɪŋɡ!〕n. 一元美鈔
parking〔ˈpɑrkɪŋ〕n. 停車
fee〔fi〕n. 費用
change〔tʃendʒ〕n. 零錢；找回的餘錢
popcorn〔ˈpɑp͵kɔrn〕n. 爆米花
quarter〔ˈkwɔrtɚ〕n. 二角五分

35. *You have to pay in advance.*

Dialogue 1

A : This is a great apartment.
這是一間很好的公寓。

B : I'm glad you like it. 我很高興你喜歡它。

A : I only hope I can afford it.
我只希望我負擔得起。

B : Well, I require the first and last month's rent and a damage deposit.
噢，我要求第一個月付兩個月的房租以及損壞押租。

A : How much does all that come to?
那總共多少錢？

B : $650, and you have to pay in advance.
六百五十元，而你必須預先付錢。

Dialogue 2

A : Did you see the ad for the new play?
你有沒有看到這齣新戲的廣告？

B : Yes, it should be excellent.
有啊，應該很棒吧。

A : Shall we plan on seeing it?
我們打算去看嗎？

B : Sure, how about going on opening night?
好啊，開演的那一晚去如何？

A : Terrific idea. 好主意。

B : I'd better call and reserve the tickets in advance.
我最好預先打電話去訂票。

Dialogue 3

A : What are all those things in your office?
　　你辦公室裏的那些東西是什麼？

B : I'm going to Chicago for a sales meeting next month.
　　下個月我要到芝加哥參加銷售會議。

A : Are you making a presentation?
　　你要上台發表嗎？

B : Yes, and I have a lot of material to take with me.
　　是啊，因此我要帶很多資料。

A : You'd better send most of it ahead of time.
　　你最好在預定時間之前先將大部分寄出。

B : I will, or it won't get there on time.
　　我會的，否則它無法準時寄達。

〔舉一反三〕

A : Can I rent a room for the night?
　　我可以租個房間過夜嗎？

B : You'll have to pay for it in advance.
　　你必須先付錢。

A : Sally already has a date for the dance next month.
　　莎莉下個月的舞會中已經有伴了。

B : He really asked her way in advance, didn't he?
　　他很早以前就邀她，對不對？

A : Is she familiar with the contract?
　　她熟悉這契約嗎？

B : I'll speak to her in advance of the meeting.
　　我會在開會以前跟她談談。

A : John's package still hasn't arrived.

約翰的包裹仍然沒到。

B : Really? He mailed it way ahead of time.

眞的嗎？他在預定時間之前就寄出去了。

A : Why weren't you here on time?

你爲什麼沒有準時到呢？

B : I needed more advance notice.

我需要更多的事先通知。

【註釋】

afford〔ə'ford,ə'fɔrd〕vt. 力足以負擔～

require〔rɪ'kwaɪr〕vt. 需要；要求

rent〔rɛnt〕n. 租金

the first and last months rent 在美國租房子，通常房東要求第一個月初先付二個月的租金。從第二個月起，每月初房客依規定付該月所應付之租金，如果房客有意退租，須卅天以前給房東一個通知，即所謂的 30 days' notice 也就是說這是房客租房子的最後一個月，而這個月房客不用付房租，因他第一個月已付過了。

damage deposit 損壞押租　　*in advance* 預先

ad = advertisement〔͵ædvə'taɪzmənt〕n. 廣告

play〔ple〕n. 戲劇

terrific〔tə'rɪfɪk〕*adj.* 非常棒的；好極了

reserve〔rɪ'zɝv〕vt. 預訂（座位，房間，機票）

presentation〔͵prɛzn̩'teʃən〕n. 表現；發表

material〔mə'tɪrɪəl〕n. 資料　　*ahead of time* 在預定時刻前

on time 準時　　date〔det〕n. 約會的對方

familiar〔fə'mɪljə〕*adj.* 熟悉的　　package〔'pækɪdʒ〕n. 包裹

36. Can you give me a hand?

Dialogue 1

A : Are you busy, Al?
你忙嗎，阿爾？

B : No, I'm not. Why?
不，我不忙。幹什麼？

A : Can you give me a hand with this chair?
你能幫我搬一下這張椅子嗎？

B : Sure. What are you trying to do?
好的。你想怎麼樣呢？

A : I want to put it on the other side of the room.
我想把它放在房間的另一邊。

B : Sure, I'll help you.
好的，我會幫你的忙。

Dialogue 2

A : What do you want, John?
約翰，你想幹什麼？

B : Can you give me a hand with my English homework?
你能幫我做英文作業嗎？

A : What do you have to do? 你要做什麼？

B : I have to write a composition.
我必須寫一篇作文。

A : You should be able to do that by yourself.
你應該自己可以做啊。

B : I know, but I don't know what to write about.
我知道，不過我不知道該寫些什麼。

Dialogue 3

A : Well, the last guest just left!
　　噢，最後一位客人才剛走！

B : The party was really a success!
　　這次的宴會眞是成功！

A : Everyone seemed to be having a good time.
　　每個人似乎都很愉快。

B : I'm really tired, but I don't want to leave this mess until morning.
　　我眞累，不過我不想把這亂七八糟的東西擱到早上再處理。

A : Let's clean it up now. I'll give you a hand.
　　我們現在就來清理吧。我會幫你忙。

B : Why don't you start the dishes and I'll vacuum.
　　那你就開始洗碗，而我來吸灰塵。

〔舉一反三〕

A : This bag is really heavy.
　　這袋子眞重。

B : Just a minute, I'll give you a hand.
　　等一下，我來幫你忙。

A : I need some help with my packages.
　　我需要人來幫我提包裹。

B : If you can wait, I'll give you a hand with them.
　　如果你肯等一下，我就可以幫你的忙。

A : Can you give me a hand with this basket?
　　你肯幫我提這籃子嗎？

B : Sure. I'd be glad to.
　　好的。我很樂意。

A : Let me give you a hand with that suitcase.
　　讓我幫你提那手提箱。

B : Thanks. It's heavier than I thought.
　　謝了。它比我想像中要重。

A : Did someone help you with your homework?
　　有人幫你做家庭作業嗎？

B : Yes, my dad gave me a hand.
　　有的，我爸爸幫我的忙。

【註釋】

give sb. a hand 幫忙某人
homework〔'hom,wɜk〕*n.* 家庭作業
composition〔,kɑmpə'zɪʃən〕*n.* 作文
have a good time 過得愉快；玩得痛快
mess〔mɛs〕*n.* 骯髒的一堆；雜亂的一團，亂七八糟的一團
clean up 使潔淨；整理
vacuum〔'vækjʊəm〕*vi.* 用吸塵器打掃
suitcase〔'sut,kes，'sjut,kes〕*n.* 手提箱

Can you give me a hand with my English homework?

What do you want, John?

37. Stick around.

Dialogue 1

A : I'm going home now.

我現在要回家了。

B : Stick around. We're going to watch *Dallas*.

再多待一會兒嘛。我們要看「朱門恩怨」呢。

A : Is that on tonight?

是今晚演的嗎？

B : Yes. It's Friday.

是啊，今天是星期五。

A : O.K., I'll stay for the show.

好吧，那我就留下來看這個節目。

B : Good. We'll make some popcorn.

好極了。我們要做些爆米花。

Dialogue 2

A : This party is really boring.

這次宴會真無聊。

B : It sure is. 的確如此。

A : Let's leave.

我們走吧。

B : No, not yet. Let's stick around until they serve the food.

不，別走。讓我們待到食物上場。

A : Good idea. 好主意。

B : Sure, then we'll leave.

當然，然後我們再走。

Dialogue 3

A : How are you doing with your math homework?
你的數學家庭作業做得如何？

B : Not very well.
不很好。

A : If you stick around, I'll help you with it.
如果你等一下，我就可以幫你的忙。

B : Thanks.
謝謝。

A : Just wait until I finish my own work.
只要等我做完自己的工作就行。

B : I've got plenty of time.
我有很多時間。

〔 **舉一反三** 〕

A : What are you going to do now?
你現在要做什麼？

B : Stick around and you'll find out.
再等一下你就知道了。

A : If you stick around ten minutes, I'll give you a ride.
如果你再待十分鐘，我就送你一程。

B : Thanks, I will.
謝謝，我會的。

A : Are you in a hurry?
你在趕時間嗎？

B : No, I can stick around for a while.
不，我可以再逗留一會兒。

A : When's dinner?
　　什麼時候吃晚飯？

B : Stick around. It's almost ready.
　　再等一下。就快好了。

A : I'm leaving. I can't hang around here all day.
　　我要走了。我不能整天都在這裏閒晃。

B : Don't leave yet. The program is about to start.
　　別走。節目就快開始了。

【註釋】

　　stick around 在附近逗留或等待
　　boring (ˈborɪŋ) *adj.* 無聊的
　　plenty of 許多的
　　hang around 留在附近；閒晃；無所事事

38. *I like the soaps.*

Dialogue 1

A : What's your favorite pastime?
你最喜歡的消遣是什麼？
B : I like to watch TV.
我喜歡看電視。

A : What TV programs do you like?
你喜歡哪些電視節目呢？
B : I like the soaps. What do you like?
我喜歡看連續劇。你喜歡做些什麼呢？

A : I like photography.
我喜歡攝影。
B : I do, too, but it costs too much.
我也是，不過那要花太多錢了。

Dialogue 2

A : Daytime television is really boring.
白天的電視真是無聊。
B : Oh, I don't agree. 噢，我不同意。

A : There's nothing on all day but soap operas.
整天除了連續劇之外沒有別的。
B : Some of the soaps are really interesting.
有些連續劇真的很有趣。

A : You must be kidding!
你一定是在開玩笑！
B : No, I'm not. I'm a fan of *General Hospital*.
不，我沒有。我是「綜合醫院」的電視迷呢。

Dialogue 3

A : What's a soap opera?
　　什麼叫肥皂劇？

B : Oh, it's a continuing, daily TV drama.
　　噢，它是一種每天放映的電視連續劇。

A : But why is it called a "soap?"
　　可是為什麼會叫做「肥皂」劇呢？

B : That's from the commercials.
　　那是由廣告而來的。

A : Commercials? 廣告？

B : Yes. Most of the shows used to be sponsored by
　　soap companies, hence the term "soap operas."
　　是啊。大部分這些節目通常是由肥皂廠商贊助，所以有「肥皂劇」這
　　個名詞。

〔舉一反三〕

A : Do you watch daytime TV?
　　你看白天的電視節目嗎？

B : No, there's nothing on but soaps.
　　沒有，除了連續劇外沒有別的。

A : Poor Joan, she's having so many family problems.
　　可憐的喬安，她有很多的家庭問題。

B : I know. Her life is like a soap opera.
　　我知道。她的一生就像是一齣連續劇。

A : What's the rush?
　　急什麼？

B : I have to get home. My favorite soap is on at one.
　　我得回家了。我最喜歡的連續劇一點鐘開始演。

A : Do you watch *General Hospital*?
　　你看過「綜合醫院」嗎？

B : No, I hate soap operas.
　　沒有，我討厭連續劇。

A : What's on TV?
　　電視在演什麼？

B : Nothing but talk shows and soaps.
　　除了脫口秀和肥皂劇外沒有別的。

《背景說明》

　　soap 在此指連續劇，起源是因為早期的連續劇，是由賣肥皂的廠商所是供的節目（ soap opera ），因此沿用下來，soap 就成了連續劇的通俗稱呼。

　　如果要問別人喜歡哪個電視節目，就說：What kind of TV program do you like?

【註釋】

pastime〔'pæs,taɪm,'pɑs,taɪm〕*n.* 消遣；娛樂
program〔'progræm〕*n.* 節目
soap〔sop〕*n.* 連續劇　　photography〔fə'tɑgrəfɪ〕*n.* 攝影
daytime〔'de,taɪm〕*n.* 日間；白晝
soap opera 連續劇（即報紙娛樂版上常用「肥皂劇」來表示）
You're kidding! 你在開玩笑吧！
commercial〔kə'mɝʃəl〕*n.* 電台或電視的廣告
shows〔ʃoz〕*n.* 演出；戲劇；電影馬戲團；（電視的）節目
talk shows 訪問性的節目（報紙娛樂版上常用「脫口秀」來表示）
sponsor〔'spɑnsɚ〕*n.*（電台或電視廣告的）贊助者；提供者
hence〔hɛns〕*adv.* 因此；所以；從此　　term〔tɝm〕*n.* 名詞；術語

39. I'm an average player.

Dialogue 1

A : Do you like to play tennis?
你喜歡打網球嗎?

B : It's my favorite sport.
那是我最喜歡的運動。

A : Do you play often?
你常打嗎?

B : I play for an hour every morning.
我每天早上打一個小時。

A : Are you a good player?
那你是個好手囉?

B : No, just an average player.
不,只是普通而已。

Dialogue 2

A : I hear Jean plays the piano.
我聽說琴彈鋼琴。

B : Yes, she does. 是的,她彈鋼琴。

A : Has she been playing long?
她彈很久了嗎?

B : For about four years.
大約有四年了。

A : She must be good.
那她一定不錯了。

B : Well, she's about average. Give her time.
嗯,她大概只是普通而已。給她時間吧。

Dialogue 3

A : Ready for our date, Bob?
  準備要赴約了嗎？鮑伯。

B : Yes, I am. Did you decide which discotheque you wanted to go to?
  是的，我準備好了。你決定要去哪一家舞廳了嗎？

A : Yeah. How does Black Cat's sound?
  是的。「黑貓」如何？

B : Fine, but don't expect too much. I'm only an average dancer.
  好的，但是別期望太高。我跳得不怎麼樣。

A : It's O.K. So am I!
  沒關係。我也是！

B : What time do you want to leave?
  你幾點要出發？

〔舉一反三〕

A : Do you play tennis well?
  你網球打得好嗎？

B : I'm an average player.
  普通而已。

A : You must be expert at golf.
  你一定是高爾夫球的行家。

B : No, I'm just an average player.
  不，只是普通而已。

A : How well can he speak English?
  他英語說得如何？

B : He's about average.
  普通。

A : Is he good at table tennis?

他擅長打桌球嗎?

B : No, he's just a beginner.

不,他只是個初學者。

A : Are you a big drinker?

你是個豪飲的酒徒嗎?

B : I would say I'm a moderate drinker.

我倒寧願說我是個有節制的飲酒者。

【註釋】

tennis (ˈtɛnɪs) n. 網球

average (ˈævərɪdʒ) adj. 普通的;平常的

discotheque (ˌdɪskəˈtek) n. 迪斯可舞廳

be expert at 熟練於;精通於;成爲~的專家

· golf (gɑlf, gɔlf) n. 高爾夫球

table tennis 乒乓球;桌球

moderate (ˈmɑdərɪt) adj. 有節制的;適度的

It's my favorite sport.

Do you like to play tennis?

40. We have thirty minutes to kill.

Dialogue 1

A : The train won't leave for another thirty minutes.
這火車要再過三十分鐘才開。

B : That gives us half an hour to kill. What do you want to do?
那給了我們半個小時消遣。你想要做什麼？

A : Let's go have coffee.
我們去喝咖啡吧。

B : And buy some magazines.
還要買些雜誌。

A : We don't have time to do both.
我們沒有時間兩樣都做。

B : O.K. Let's just have coffee.
好吧，那我們只喝咖啡就行了。

Dialogue 2

A : Why aren't you busy?
你爲什麼不忙？

B : I finished all my work.
我把所有的工作都做完了。

A : Why are you just sitting there?
你爲什麼只是坐在那裏？

B : I'm just killing time until lunch begins.
我只是在打發時間等開午飯。

A : The boss will be angry if he catches you.
　　如果讓老闆逮到你的話，他會生氣的。

B : He won't. He left early for lunch.
　　他不會的。他提早離開去吃午飯了。

Dialogue 3

A : Don't you have any ambition?
　　你沒有雄心壯志嗎？

B : Sure. Why do you ask?
　　當然有啊。你爲什麼要問呢？

A : Why are you working as a busboy?
　　那你爲什麼要到餐廳收盤碗打工呢？

B : I'm just killing time until I go into the army.
　　我只是打發時間等入伍。

A : When will that be?
　　什麼時候啊？

B : Next month.
　　下個月。

〔舉一反三〕

A : Why were you talking to that girl?
　　你爲什麼要跟那個女孩子說話？

B : I was just killing time until you got here.
　　我只是打發時間等你。

A : The president won't arrive until three o'clock.
　　董事長要三點才會來。

B : We have some time to kill. Let's go have coffee.
　　我們還有時間消磨。我們去喝杯咖啡吧。

A : Why are those workers just standing around?
　　爲什麼那些工人只站在那裏？

B : They're killing time until their workshift starts.
　　他們在打發時間等輪班。

A : We have some time to kill before the train leaves.
　　在火車開動之前我們還有一些時間可以打發。

B : Let's go buy some magazines.
　　我們去買些雜誌吧。

A : Oh no, we missed our train!
　　哎呀，我們錯過火車了！

B : That means we have an hour to kill before the next one.
　　那表示在下班火車來之前，我們還要消磨一個小時。

【註釋】

kill〔kɪl〕*vt.* 消遣；打發
boss〔bɔs〕*n.* 老板
ambition〔æm'bɪʃən〕*n.* 野心；雄心；抱負
busboy〔'bʌs,bɔɪ〕*n.* 餐廳收碗盤之打雜工人
president〔'prɛzədənt〕*n.* 總經理；董事長；大學校長；總統（通常字首大寫）
workshift 輪班值勤時間；值班

41. Whatever you say.

Dialogue 1

A : How about having dinner together after work tonight?
今晚工作完成後一起去吃晚飯如何？

B : Fine.
好啊。

A : Shall we have Chinese or American food?
我們要吃中式還是美式餐飲？

B : Whatever you say.
隨便你。

A : There's a good beef noodle house around the corner.
轉角有家不錯的牛肉麵館。

B : Oh, I'm sorry, but I'm a vegetarian.
噢，真抱歉，我是吃素的。

Dialogue 2

A : You're the computer expert, what's wrong?
你是電腦專家，有什麼差錯？

B : Terminal 16 is down.
十六號終端機壞了。

A : Whatever you say, as long as it's fixed by tomorrow.
不管你怎麼說，只要它在明天以前修好就行了。

B : I'll call the repair service right away.
我會馬上打電話叫修護服務站。

A : I hope it's nothing serious.
我希望沒什麼嚴重的情形發生。

B : I hope so, too. 我也是希望如此。

Dialogue 3

A : I finally got that promotion!
　　我終於獲得升遷了！

B : I'm so proud of you.
　　我真以你為榮。

A : We should go somewhere for the weekend to celebrate.
　　這個週末我們該找個地方慶祝一番。

B : Whatever you say--you won the promotion.
　　你怎麼說都行——反正你已經獲得升遷了。

A : Well, let's drive down to the beach.
　　嗯，那我們開車到海濱。

B : Sounds like a good idea.
　　好像是個好主意。

〔舉一反三〕

A : I've decided to buy a stereo instead of that used car.
　　我已經決定買一套立體音響設備而不買那輛舊車。

B : Whatever you say--it's your money.
　　隨便你——那是你的錢。

A : Would you mind if we left on Saturday morning instead of Friday afternoon?
　　如果我們星期六早上走而不是星期五下午走，你會介意嗎？

B : Whatever you say.
　　隨便你。

A : I can give you $12,000 a year to start with.
　　我可以給你一年一萬二千元起薪。

B : Whatever you say. 你怎麼說都行。

A : Whatever you decide is all right with me.
　　無論你怎麼決定，我都同意。

B : Fine, then we'll take the blue one.
　　好吧，那麼我們就拿藍色的。

A : Whatever you think is right will probably be O.K.
　　with me.
　　只要你認爲是對的，我大概也會同意。

B : All right, I'll give you an answer in the morning.
　　好的，我早上給你答覆。

【註釋】

Whatever you say. 你怎麼說都行；隨便你。
beef noodle 牛肉麵
vegetarian (ˌvɛdʒəˈtɛrɪən) *n.* 素食者
terminal (ˈtɝmənl̩) *n.* （電腦的）終端機
stereo (ˈstɛrɪo, ˈstɪrɪo) *n.* 立體音響設備

Oh, I'm sorry, but I'm a vegetarian.

There's a good beef noodle house around the corner.

42. It'll come to me.

Dialogue 1

A : Do you remember the name of the man we met at
the restaurant?
你還記得我們在餐廳裏遇到的那個人的名字嗎?

B : Which man? 哪個人?

A : The man with red hair. 紅頭髮的那一個。

B : Oh, him. No, I don't remember his name.
噢,他啊。不,我不記得他的名字了。

A : It was a common name. Started with a K, I think.
那是個普通的名字。我想是 K 開頭。

B : Oh, yes. Just a minute, it'll come to me.
噢,是的。等一下,我會想起來的。

Dialogue 2

A : What's the license number of your car?
你的汽車駕照號碼是多少?

B : Oh, dear. Let me think a minute.
噢,老天。讓我想想。

A : You just told me yesterday.
你昨天才剛告訴我的。

B : I know, but it's slipped my mind.
我知道,不過我忘了。

A : It starts with a zero, doesn't it?
零開頭的,對不對?

B : Just a minute. It'll come to me.
等一下,我會想起來的。

Dialogue 3

A : This picture reminds me of something.
這幅畫讓我想起了一樣東西。

B : Me too, but I can't think what.
我也是，不過我想不起來是什麼了。

A : Something to do with the colors.
跟顏色有關的。

B : Let me think. Maybe it'll come to me.
讓我想想。也許我會記起來。

A : Oh, I know! Our trip to Mexico!
噢，我知道了！我們到墨西哥的旅行！

B : Right! All those bright colors at the fiesta.
對了！祭典時的那些鮮豔的彩帶。

〔舉一反三〕

A : What's his name?
他叫什麼名字？

B : Let me think. It'll come to me.
讓我想想。我會記起來的。

A : Do you remember her phone number?
你記得她的電話號碼嗎？

B : I should. Just a minute, it'll come to me.
應該記得。等一下，我會記起來的。

A : Who does he remind you of?
他使你想起了誰？

B : Let me see. Someone I know very well. Just a
minute, it'll come to me.
讓我想想。一個我很熟的人。等一下，我會記起來的。

A：How much did your vacation cost?

　你這次假期花了多少錢？

B：My husband told me, but I've forgotten. Wait, it'll come to me.

　我先生跟我講過，不過我已經忘了。等等，我快想起來了。

A：Weren't you going to tell me something?

　你不是要告訴我什麼事嗎？

B：Yes, but I've forgotten what it was. Just a minute, it'll come to me.

　是啊，不過我已經忘了是什麼。等一下，我快想起來了。

【註釋】

come to 憶及

color（'kʌlɚ）*n.*（*pl.*）　色彩；彩帶

bright〔braɪt〕*adj.* 鮮豔的；明亮的

fiesta〔fɪ'ɛstə〕*n.* 假日；宗教之節日祭典；聖徒之紀念日

43. *I'm just about to leave.*

Dialogue 1

A : Are you still here?
你還在嗎?

B : I'm just about to leave.
我正要走。

A : Did you have some extra work to do?
你有額外的工作要做嗎?

B : Yes. The manager had me inventory today's shipment.
是的。經理要我清點今天的進貨。

A : Well, I'll see you tomorrow.
好吧,那明天再見囉。

B : Good night. See you tomorrow.
晚安。明天見。

Dialogue 2

A : Hello. Is Mr. Smith there?
喂,史密斯先生在嗎?

B : Jean? Hi, it's me, Bob.
琴嗎?嗨,是我啊,鮑伯。

A : Bob! I thought you were going to meet me here at six!
鮑伯!我以為你六點就會來見我。

B : I know. I'm sorry, Jean, but something came up. I was just about to leave when you called.
我知道。抱歉,琴,不過是因為發生了一些事情。當妳打電話來時,我正要走。

A : So I'll see you in about fifteen minutes?

那麼再過十五分鐘我就可以見到你了嗎?

B : Right. Bye.

是的。再見。

Dialogue 3

A : Did you see Sue?

你見到蘇了嗎?

B : Yes. She's very upset.

是的。她很難過。

A : I know! She looked like she was just about to cry.

我知道!她看起來就像馬上要哭的樣子。

B : Poor girl. Her favorite aunt just died.

可憐的孩子。她最喜歡的阿姨剛過世。

A : Let's come by tomorrow to cheer her up.

明天之前我們去安慰她吧。

B : That's a good idea.

好主意。

〔舉一反三〕

A : Is Jean still here?

琴還在嗎?

B : Yes, but you'd better hurry. She was just about to leave. 是的,不過你最好快一點。她馬上要走了。

A : What would you like to hear? This record is just about over.

你想聽什麼?這唱片快放完了。

B : The other side would be fine.

另外一面就可以了。

A : The end of the term is just about here. Have you finished your paper?

期限就快到了。你的作業做完了沒有？

B : I'm just about through.

我快做完了。

A : This movie's just about over.

電影快完了。

B : Let's leave now and beat the crowd.

我們現在穿過群眾離開吧。

A : You look upset. What's wrong?

你看起來很難過的樣子。怎麼了？

B : I hate my work. I've just about had enough of that supervisor of mine.

我討厭我的工作。我受夠了我的主管。

【註釋】

be about to 正要（用於表即將發生的動作）

extra〔'ɛkstrə〕*adj.* 額外的

inventory〔'ɪnvənˌtorɪ , 'ɪnvənˌtɔrɪ〕*vt.* 清點存貨；編列詳細目錄

shipment〔'ʃɪpmənt〕*n.* 載貨；船貨；裝貨；出貨

upset〔ʌp'sɛt〕*adj.* 難過的

cheer *sb.* **up** 鼓勵某人

beat〔bit〕*vt.* 開路

term〔tɝm〕*n.* 期限；期間

supervisor〔ˌsjupɚ'vaɪzɚ〕*n.* 監督者；管理人；指導人；主管

44. *You name it.*

Dialogue 1

A : You'll really like the food here!
你真的會喜歡這裏的食物！

B : The menu is enormous.
菜單上真是種類繁多。

A : Yes, they have an excellent selection.
是啊，他們都要精挑細選一番。

B : They even have snails!
他們甚至連蝸牛都有！

A : You name it and they probably have it.
你叫得出來的他們大概就會有。

B : How about just a plain hamburger?
來一客不加其他東西的漢堡如何？

Dialogue 2

A : This department store is huge!
這家百貨公司真大！

B : I know. They have everything here.
我知道。他們這裏什麼都有。

A : Everything? 什麼都有？

B : Sure. You name it and they've got it.
是啊。只要你叫得出口，他們都有。

A : How about an elephant?
那麼來隻大象如何？

B : A toy elephant, yes.
有啊，玩具象。

Dialogue 3

A : Choose a toy, Sally. Anything you want.
挑一樣玩具吧，莎莉。你要什麼都可以。
B : Anything I want?
我要什麼都行？

A : You name it, it's yours.
你說出來，就是你的。
B : Just one?
只有一樣嗎？

A : Yes, just one.
是的，只能一樣。
B : I want that doll.
我要那個娃娃。

〔舉一反三〕

A : Can I really have whatever I want?
我真的要什麼都行嗎？
B : Sure. You name it, it's yours.
是啊。只要你說出來，就是你的。

A : How many kinds of tools do you have, Mr. Smith?
你有多少種工具，史密斯先生？
B : All kinds. You name it, I have it.
所有的種類都有。只要你說得出口，我都有。

A : Can I get a ring made like this one?
我能有一只做像這樣的戒指嗎？
B : You just tell me what you want and I'll make it.
你只要告訴我你要什麼樣子，我就可以做得出來。

A : Can I have a party on my birthday?
　　我生日的時候可以開個舞會嗎？

B : You can have whatever you want.
　　你要怎麼樣都行。

A : I need to reserve four tables for lunch.
　　我要預訂四張桌子吃午餐。

B : Whatever you say, sir.
　　先生，請您儘管吩咐。

【註釋】

enormous (ɪ'nɔrməs) *adj.* 極大的；龐大的
selection (sə'lɛkʃən) *n.* 選擇；挑選
snail (snel) *n.* 蝸牛
plain (plen) *adj.* 普通的；一般的；在此指「不加其他東西的」
hamburger ('hæmbɝɡɚ) *n.* 漢堡
You name it. 你說得出名字；你叫得出口。
ring (rɪŋ) *n.* 戒指

Choose a toy, Sally. Anything you want.

I want that doll.

45. *If I were in your shoes.*

Dialogue 1

A : Are you really quitting your job?
你眞的要辭去你的工作嗎?

B : Well, what would you do if you were in my shoes?
嗯,如果你站在我的立場,你會怎麼做?

A : What did they do that was so bad?
他們倒底做了什麼事,這麼糟糕?

B : They wanted me to take a cut in pay.
他們要削減我的薪水。

A : Then if I were in your shoes, I'd do the same thing.
如果我站在你的立場,我也會這麼做。

B : Thanks for the support.
謝謝你對我的支持。

Dialogue 2

A : I hope I did the right thing.
希望我沒做錯事。

B : What happened? 出了什麼事?

A : I had some tests done at the hospital and they lost the results.
我在醫院裏做了檢查,而他們卻把結果搞丟了。

B : What did you do? 那你怎麼辦?

A : I insisted that they run the tests again at no extra charge. 我堅持要他們不額外收費,再替我檢查一次。

B : If I had been in your shoes, I'd have done the same thing. 如果我換成你的話,我也會這樣做。

Dialogue 3

A : I'd hate to be the boss.
　　我討厭當老板。
B : Why?
　　為什麼？

A : All those decisions, all that responsibility.
　　所有的那些決定，所有的責任。
B : Yeah, it's really a tough job.
　　是啊，這的確是件很困難的工作。

A : If I were in his shoes, I'd probably have a nervous
breakdown.
　　如果我是老板的話，我可能會精神崩潰。
B : You don't have to worry. You'll never be boss.
　　你用不著操心。你永遠當不了老板。

〔 **舉一反三** 〕

A : I'm leaving town.
　　我要出城了。
B : If I were in your shoes, I'd do the same thing.
　　如果我站在你的立場，我也會這樣做。

A : If you were in my shoes, would you accept this job?
　　如果你站在我的立場，你會不會接受這份工作？
B : Probably not.
　　也許不會。

A : What would your foreign policy be, if you were in
Ronald Reagan's shoes?
　　如果你站在隆納德·雷根的立場，你的外交政策會是如何？
B : I have no idea.
　　我不知道。

A : If you were in my position, would you accept this job?

如果你站在我的立場，你會不會接受這份工作？

B : No, I wouldn't.

不，我不會。

A : If you were in my situation, would you accept this job?

如果你處在我的立場，你會不會接受這份工作？

B : No, I wouldn't.

不，我不會。

《背景說明》

be in *one's* **shoes** 從字面上的意思「穿著某人的鞋子」，可以體會出它的涵意是「站在某人的立場」，這裡的 shoes 是 position 或 place 的意思。而且說這話的時候，都是一種假設的情況，因此當然要用 if I *were* in your shoes（與現在事實相反的假設）或 if I *had been* in your shoes（與過去事實相反的假設）。

【註釋】

be in *one's* **shoes** 處於某人的立場；換成是某人

cut〔kʌt〕*n.* 降低；減少

pay〔pe〕*n.* 薪資；工資

test〔tɛst〕*n.* 檢驗；考驗

charge〔tʃɑrdʒ〕*n.* 費用；索價

responsibility〔rɪˌspɑnsə'bɪlətɪ〕*n.* 責任

tough〔tʌf〕*adj.* 費力的；困難的

nervous breakdown 精神崩潰

46. *She's a born singer.*

Dialogue 1

A : Did you hear Jennifer at the party last night?
　　昨天晚上的宴會裏你有沒有聽到珍妮佛在唱歌?

B : Yes. She has a beautiful voice.
　　有啊。她有一副好嗓子。

A : And she isn't shy about singing in public, either.
　　而且她也不會羞於在公衆之前唱歌。

B : Jennifer is a born singer.
　　珍妮佛眞是一位天生的歌手。

A : I agree. Does she plan to sing professionally?
　　我同意。她打算要唱職業的嗎?

B : She should, she's very talented.
　　應該會的,她很有天份。

Dialogue 2

A : Our daughter's recital was wonderful.
　　我們女兒的獨奏會表演得好極了。

B : It sure was. Do you know what her teacher said?
　　的確不錯。你知道她的老師說了什麼嗎?

A : No, what?
　　不知道,她說什麼?

B : She said Jane was a born pianist.
　　她說珍是個天生的鋼琴家。

A : We should encourage her.
　　我們應該要鼓勵她。

B : Yes, we should. 是的,那是應該的。

Dialogue 3

A : What a wonderful cast!
演員的陣容真強！

B : Yes, some people are born actors.
是啊，有些人簡直是天生的演員。

A : And others work at it very hard.
而其他的人卻很難辦到。

B : We should come to the movies more often.
我們應該更常去看電影。

A : They're showing *The Sound of Music* at the Hoover.
豪華戲院正在放映「真善美」。

B : That sounds good.
似乎不錯。

〔 舉一反三 〕

A : Susan has a beautiful voice.
蘇珊有副好嗓子。

B : Yes. She's a born singer.
是的。她是個天生的歌手。

A : The champ won again.
冠軍又贏了。

B : Yes. He's a natural-born fighter.
是啊。他簡直就像是天生的拳擊手。

A : All those Browns sing so well.
布朗一家人都很會唱歌。

B : It runs in the family. They're born musicians.
那是這一家人的特性、他們是天生的音樂家。

A : I think Tom will make the team.
　　我認為湯姆會中選入隊。

B : So do I. He's a natural athlete.
　　我也這麼想。他是位天生的運動員。

A : Mary was cut out to be a nurse.
　　瑪麗適合當護士。

B : I think so, too.
　　我也認為如此。

《背景説明》

　　She's a born singer (*or **musician, pianist, TV star, actress,***
…). 是用來稱讚別人的話，其中的 born 和 natural-born 意思相似，
都表示「天生的；與生俱來的」。這句話通常在別人表現得很不錯的時
候使用，如果一個人表現平平，説這句話就顯得奉承或阿諛。至於在別
人表現不佳時，説這句話就成了諷刺或挖苦了。

【註釋】

in public 公開地；公然　　born〔bɔrn〕*adj.* 天生的
professionally〔prə'fɛʃnəlɪ〕*adv.* 職業地；專業地
talented〔'tæləntɪd〕*adj.* 有才能的
recital〔rɪ'saɪtḷ〕*n.* 獨奏會；獨唱會　　pianist〔'pɪənɪst〕*n.* 鋼琴家
encourage〔ɪn'kɝɪdʒ〕*vt.* 鼓勵　　cast〔kæst, kɑst〕*n.* 演員的陣容；卡司
run in the family 家族共同的特性；家族遺傳得來
natural-born〔'nætʃərəl'bɔrn〕*adj.* 天生的
athlete〔'æθlit〕*n.* 運動員；運動家　　***be cut out to be*** ~ 適合當~
make the team 中選入隊。如 Tom 棒球打得很好，他爭取參加學校的棒
　　球隊，你覺得他會入選而參加球隊，你就可説：Tom will make the
　　baseball team.

47. I'll play it by ear.

Dialogue 1

A : I'm so glad the weekend's finally here.
很高興週末終於來了。

B : Me, too. I'm going out tonight.
我也是。我今天晚上要出去。

A : Where are you going to go?
你要去哪兒？

B : I don't know. I'll play it by ear.
我不知道。隨興之所至吧。

A : Sometimes that's more fun!
有時候，這樣子反而更好玩！

B : I think so, too.
我也這麼認為。

Dialogue 2

A : Are you leaving for Europe soon?
你快要去歐洲了嗎？

B : In two weeks. 還有兩個禮拜。

A : Have you decided where you're going?
你有沒有決定去哪些地方？

B : I'll play it by ear when I get there.
到了那邊再看情形。

A : That sounds exciting. Have a good trip.
好像很刺激。祝你旅途愉快。

B : Thanks. I hope to.
謝謝。希望如此。

Dialogue 3

A : Hi Sam, are you ready for class?
嗨，山姆，功課都準備了沒？

B : No, I forgot to finish the speech I'm supposed to give today.
還沒，我忘了準備好今天應該發表的演講。

A : Aren't you concerned about it?
難道你不擔心嗎？

B : No, I'll just play it by ear.
不會，我到時隨機應變。

A : Well, you talk a lot, you should do O.K.!
嗯，你一向多話，應該沒問題！

B : You're right! Sometimes being a chatterbox can come in handy.
不錯！有時做個話匣子多少也有些用處。

〔舉一反三〕

A : Aren't you going to prepare a speech for the program?
難道你對這個計畫不準備發表意見嗎？

B : No, I'll just play it by ear.
不用，我隨機應變就行了。

A : Have you and Joe made definite plans for your vacation? 你和喬對你們的假期有沒有明確的計畫？

B : No, we'll just play it by ear.
沒有，到時候走到哪兒玩到哪兒。

A : How did you know what to say to him?
你怎麼知道要跟他說什麼？

B : I didn't. I just played it by ear.
我不知道。我只不過是臨機應對罷了。

A : Did you follow any special plan when you designed this room?

當你們在設計這房間的時候,有沒有用什麼特別的計畫?

B : No, we just played it by ear.

沒有,我們只是隨興之所至。

A : How are you going to tell your parents that you failed the examination?

你要怎麼跟你父母親說你考試不及格?

B : I don't know. I'll just have to play it by ear.

我不知道。我只有隨機應變了。

《 背景説明 》

　　play it by ear 原意是「隨著耳朵喜歡聽什麼曲調,就彈什麼曲調,不預先安排」,引申為做事沒有預先安排,隨機或隨興而變,是一種非正式的用法,可以用在任何情況。

【註釋】

play it by ear 隨機應變;看情形再說;事先不計畫,隨興之所至而定
concern about 擔憂;關心
chatterbox ('tʃætəˌbɑks) *n.* 饒舌者
come in handy 隨時都會有用處

48. *You should take advantage of it.*

Dialogue 1

A : BCM International just offered me a job.
　　BCM 國際公司剛提供給我一個工作機會。

B : Are you going to take it?
　　你去不去呢？

A : Well, the pay and hours are great, and the office is pretty close.
　　嗯，薪水和工作時間都不錯，而且辦公室離我住的地方很近。

B : I think you should take advantage of it.
　　我覺得你該好好的把握這個機會。

A : Maybe so, but I'll have to think about it some more.
　　或許會吧，不過我還要再考慮一下。

B : I'm sure you'll make the right decision.
　　我相信你會做正確的決定。

Dialogue 2

A : I hear it's going to be a mild and sunny weekend.
　　聽說將有一個溫和晴朗的週末。

B : Why don't we take advantage of it to get in a round of golf?
　　我們為什麼不好好利用機會去打一回合高爾夫球？

A : Well, I promised the kids I'd take them on a picnic.
　　唉！我答應孩子要帶他們去野餐。

B : On Saturday or Sunday?
　　星期六或星期天？

A : On Sunday. I'll tell you what, let's play nine holes on Saturday afternoon.
星期天。這樣子好了，我們週六下午去打個九洞。

B : Great. I'll call you on Saturday.
好啊，我星期六再打電話給你。

Dialogue 3

A : How is Betty these days, Jim?
吉姆，貝蒂這幾天還好吧？

B : I haven't heard from her in almost two weeks.
我差不多有兩個星期沒有她的消息了。

A : Really? I thought you had really hit it off together.
真的？我一直以為你跟她相處得很好。

B : So did I, until I introduced her to my brother, Bob.
我也這麼以為，一直到我把她介紹給我的哥哥鮑伯為止。

A : It looks like she took advantage of you.
你似乎被她利用了。

B : It sure does. 的確是。

〔舉一反三〕

A : What do you think of this job offer?
你覺得這工作機會如何？

B : I think it would be to your advantage to accept.
我覺得接受這工作對你有好處。

A : Senator Brown called his opponent "over the hill and behind the times."
布朗議員說他的對手「老邁落伍」。

B : He was trying to take advantage of his challenger's age. 他只是想佔他對手年齡的便宜。

A : Look outside! The rain has stopped.
　　你看外頭！雨停了。

B : Yes, for now. Let's take advantage of it and go running.
　　是的，現在停了。我們利用這機會出去跑一跑吧。

A : Do you think she's trying to take advantage of me?
　　你認為她企圖利用我嗎？

B : No, I think she sincerely likes you.
　　不，我覺得她是眞心喜歡你。

A : I'm really gaining weight.
　　我體重眞的增加了。

B : It would be to your advantage to exercise moderately.
　　做些適度的運動，對你會有好處的。

【註釋】

take advantage of （人，事）佔（某人）便宜；利用機會
get in 加入；進行
hear from sb. 收到某人的信；得到某人的消息
hit it off 相處融洽
over the hill （爬不過山頭）體力老邁不繼
behind the times （被時間追過）落伍；思想陳腐
for now = *for the present* 現在；有「暫時」的意思

49. *How long did it last?*

Dialogue 1

A : You look tired.
你看起來累了。

B : I am. I stayed up and watched that special on TV last night.
是啊。我昨天晚上熬夜收看電視特別節目。

A : Oh, *Masada*?
哦,「瑪莎達」嗎?

B : Yes, it was excellent.
是,那節目太棒了。

A : I started to watch it, but I fell asleep. How long did it last?
剛開始我也看,可是後來睡著了。演了多久?

B : Until midnight.
一直演到午夜。

Dialogue 2

A : Did you hear?
你聽說了沒有?

B : What?
什麼事?

A : Joe was fired!
喬被開除了!

B : Again? Well, that job didn't last long!
又被開除了?哎,那工作他也沒做多久!

A : No, he was only there a month.
　　是啊，他只不過才去了一個月。

B : He's just too lazy to hold a steady job.
　　他太懶，以致不能維持一個穩定的工作。

Dialogue 3

A : What is this bill for?
　　這帳單是怎麼回事？

B : I bought Tommy some new shoes.
　　我給湯姆買了些新鞋。

A : Shoes? You just bought shoes for him last month.
　　鞋？你上個月才買鞋給他啊。

B : Well, he needed some new ones.
　　可是，他需要新鞋子。

A : His shoes don't seem to last long.
　　他的鞋子似乎穿不久。

B : He's an active, growing boy.
　　他是一個活潑，正在發育的男孩。

〔舉一反三〕

A : How long did the fight last?
　　拳擊賽進行了多久？

B : Only two rounds. The champion won.
　　只有兩回合。衛冕者贏了。

A : How long did the dance last?
　　舞會進行多久？

B : He didn't get home until three a.m.
　　他一直到清晨三點才回家。

A : I have to buy a new car.
　　我必須買輛新車。

B : How long did your old one last?
　　你那輛舊車開了多久？

A : Why are you home so early?
　　你為什麼這麼早回家？

B : The party didn't last long.
　　宴會沒有進行很久。

A : How long did those shoes last?
　　那些鞋子你穿了多久？

B : They fell apart in two months.
　　兩個月就支離破碎了。

【註釋】

last〔læst〕vi. 持續；持久

stay up 熬夜

special〔'spɛʃəl〕adj. 特別的　n. 專輯；特別節目

steady〔'stɛdɪ〕adj. 穩定的；有規律的；固定的

bill〔bɪl〕n. 帳單；鈔票

round〔raʊnd〕n. (競賽的) 一回合

fall apart 支離破碎

50. *Let's talk over coffee.*

Dialogue 1

A : Bob Jones, what a pleasant surprise running into you!
鮑伯・瓊斯，真沒想到會遇到你！

B : Mary! Long time no see! How've you been?
瑪麗！好久不見！近來好嗎？

A : Just fine. Are you busy now?
好啊，妳現在忙嗎？

B : No. I'm just killing time.
沒有，只是在打發時間。

A : There's a coffee shop near here. Let's talk over coffee. 附近有家咖啡店，我們邊喝邊聊。

B : Great. I've been thinking about you lately.
太好了，我最近一直在想妳。

Dialogue 2

A : Joe, I've got some new ideas for the company.
喬，我對公司有一些新的構想。

B : Good. I know you're always thinking ahead.
太好了，我就知道你的想法一向超前一等。

A : I think some reorganization would be good for business. 我想如果在編制上做些調整，對生意會有幫助。

B : Great. Have you eaten yet?
不錯，你吃飯了沒？

A : No, I was just on my way. 還沒，我正要去吃。

B : Fine. Then let's talk over lunch.
好，那我們一邊吃一邊談。

Dialogue 3

A : What a day! My head is killing me.
今天真累！頭痛死了。

B : You've been working hard. You should relax a little.
你工作得太辛苦了。你應該休息一下。

A : Well, I'm behind in my work and trying to catch up on it.
可是，我的工作進度落後，我正要設法趕上。

B : But it's five now and time to quit.
可是已經五點了，該下班了。

A : Do you want to talk some more over a drink?
你想不想喝杯酒再聊一聊？

B : That sounds good. Let's go.
好像不錯。走吧

〔舉一反三〕

A : Mr. Lee! What a surprise!
李先生！好難得！

B : Why don't we go somewhere and catch up on things over coffee?
我們找個地方坐，喝杯咖啡，聊一聊如何？

A : Meg, what did you decide about the BCM contract?
梅格，關於 BCM 的合約，妳決定怎麼辦？

B : I'm starved. Let's discuss it over a hamburger.
我餓死了。我們邊吃漢堡邊討論。

A : Would you like to talk about it over a drink?
你要不要邊喝酒邊談？

B : Thanks, Mike. You're such a good listener.
謝了，麥可。你真是個好聽眾。

A : Hello again. Would you like to get better acquainted over lunch?

又碰面啦！要不要一起吃午餐，多熟識一下？

B : I'd be delighted to.

我很樂意。

A : Did you talk to Mr. Lin this morning?

你今天早上有沒有和林先生談？

B : Yes. He closed the deal with the new client over dinner last night.

有。他昨天晚上用餐的時候，就完成了跟新客戶的那筆交易。

《背景説明》

　　Let's talk over coffee. 中的 over 表示「正在做某事的時候」，相當於 "while engaged in"，通常 over 之後接表示「吃、喝」方面的名詞。例如：*Let's talk over lunch* (*or a drink, dinner, a hamburger*, …). 但是也可用於其他情況，如：I heard her singing *over* her work.

【註釋】

run into （與某人）不期而遇　　*kill time* 打發時間

talk over coffee　over 在此是「正從事～的時候」，所以此句的意思是
　　「一邊喝咖啡一邊聊」天。

think ahead 想法超前一等　　*just on my way* 正要去～的路上

catch up on things　catch up 有獲得之意，on things 並不指特定
　　的事情，整句有「聊天」的意思。

starve 〔stɑrv〕*vi.*, *vt.* 飢餓　　acquaint 〔ə'kwent〕*vt.* 使熟識

be delighted to 樂意

51. Take it easy.

Dialogue 1

A : If you're free tomorrow, how about having lunch together?

如果你明天有空，一塊兒吃午餐如何？

B : Fine with me. What time shall we make it?

我沒問題。我們要約在幾點鐘？

A : Let's meet at my office at noon.

中午我們在我的辦公室碰面。

B : Fine.

好的。

A : I'll see you tomorrow then. Take it easy.

那麼明天見。再見。

B : See you tomorrow. Take care.

明兒見。保重。

Dialogue 2

A : Good morning.

早安。

B : Good morning.

早安。

A : I just wanted to touch base with you about our latest project. How's it going?

我正想跟你談談有關我們最新計畫案的基本原則。進行得如何？

B : It's moving right along. There're no problems at this point.

進行得都很順利。這點沒有問題。

A：That's good news. Well, I must go. We'll talk more about this later.
那是好消息。嗯，我得走了。關於這點，我們以後再多談些。

B：Take it easy.
再見。

Dialogue 3

A：Well, hello. How are you?
嘿，哈囉，你好嗎？

B：Oh, I'm fine. Haven't seen you in ages. Where have you been hiding yourself?
噢，我很好。很久沒見到你了。你躲到哪兒去啦？

A：I've been working long hours lately.
最近我一直長時間地工作。

B：You shouldn't be pushing yourself so hard. Take it easy.
你不該把自己逼得那麼緊，輕鬆點。

A：You're right.
你是對的。

B：Well, take care and I hope to see you again soon.
好吧，多保重，我希望不久能再見到你。

〔舉一反三〕

A：See you later.
再見。

B：Take it easy.
再見。

A：Take care. 保重。

B：You, too. 你也是。

A : We'll see you around.
我們會再見到你。

B : So long.
再見。

A : Hope to see you again. Good-bye.
希望能再見到你。再見。

B : Good-bye.
再見。

A : Looking forward to seeing you again.
希望能再見到你。

B : Same here.
我也這麼想。

【註釋】

touch〔tʌtʃ〕*vt.* 談到；論及；關涉

base〔bes〕*n.* 基本原則

project〔'pradʒɛkt〕*n.* 計畫；企畫

along〔ə'lɔŋ〕*prep.* 沿；循 *adv.* 向前；往前

ages （口語）長時間

push〔puʃ〕*vt.* 逼迫；催促；驅策

look forward to 期待；希望

Same here. = **I think so, too.** 我也這麼想。

Take it easy. 1. 放輕鬆點。 2. 再見。（此用法常用）

52. *How do you say this in English?*

Dialogue 1

A : Excuse me. Can I ask you a question?
　　對不起，我能問你一個問題嗎？

B : Sure. What is it?
　　當然可以。什麼問題？

A : How do you say this in English?
　　這樣東西用英文怎麼說？

B : We call this a "parking meter."
　　我們叫這個為「停車計費器」。

A : How do you pronounce this?
　　你們怎麼發音？

B : Parking meter.
　　〔'pɑrkɪŋ'mitɚ〕

Dialogue 2

A : How do you say discotheque in Chinese?
　　discotheque 你們中文怎麼說？

B : We don't. We just say discotheque.
　　我們不用中文說。我們就說迪斯可夜總會。

A : Oh, that's interesting.
　　噢，那很有趣。

B : There are a lot of words like that.
　　有很多字像那樣的。

A : Can you give me any examples?
　　你能舉一些例子給我嗎？
B : Sure. Club, bar, golf, and so on.
　　當然可以。俱樂部，酒吧，高爾夫球等等。

Dialogue 3

A : What's the matter? 怎麼回事？
B : I'm practicing my speech and I'm having trouble.
　　我正在練習我的演講詞，而我有了困難。

A : Anything I can help you with?
　　有我可以幫忙你的地方嗎？
B : Maybe. How do you pronounce p-s-y-c-h-i-a-t-r-y?
　　也許。你怎麼發 psychiatry 這個音？

A : Sorry, I don't know. 抱歉，我不知道。
B : Maybe I can substitute another word.
　　也許我可以用另外一個字來代替。

〔舉一反三〕

A : How do you say this in English?
　　這個你們用英文怎麼說？
B : We would say "sugar bowl." 我們說「糖罐」。

A : What do you call this in English?
　　這個你們用英文怎麼稱呼？
B : We call this a "sidewalk."
　　我們叫這做「人行道」。

A : Can you translate this into English?
　　你能把這個翻譯成英文嗎？
B : Sure. It means "It's a cinch."
　　當然。它的意思是「十拿九穩」。

A：What does that sign say in English?
　　那個標誌用英文怎麼解說？

B：It says--Parking Lot.
　　它寫著──「停車場」。

A：I can't pronounce this work correctly.
　　我沒有辦法正確地唸出這個字。

B：Place the tip of your tongue behind your upper front teeth to make the "L" sound.
　　把你的舌尖放在上顎門牙後面來發"L"的音。

《背景說明》

　　跟外國人談話的時候，難免會有一些英文單字不記得或不會唸，但至少下面幾句話要會說：*How do you say (or call) this in English?*「這個的英文怎麼說？」*How do you pronounce ~?*「~英文怎麼唸？」，否則單字不記得，又不會問，常常會使談話中斷，甚至得換個話題，豈不是很洩氣的事？

【註釋】

pronounce〔prə'naʊns〕*vt.* 唸出；發音

discotheque〔ˌdɪskə'tek〕*n.* 迪斯可夜總會（舞廳）

psychiatry〔saɪ'kaɪətrɪ〕*n.* 精神病學；精神科

substitute〔'sʌbstəˌtjut〕*vt.* 以～代替

sugar bowl 指餐桌上用的砂糖罐

sidewalk〔'saɪdˌwɔk〕*n.*〔美〕人行道。（〔英〕pavement）

translate〔træns'let〕*vt.* 翻譯

cinch〔sɪntʃ〕*n.* 易做之事或有把握之事

upper〔'ʌpɚ〕*adj.* 較高的；上部的

53. Can I get you something to drink?

Dialogue 1

A : Come on in. Have a seat, please.
進來，請坐。

B : Thank you.
謝謝你。

A : Can I get you something to drink?
我能給你拿些飲料嗎？

B : Yes. I'd like an orange juice, please.
好的，請給我一份柳橙汁。

A : Anything else?
還要其他的嗎？

B : No, thanks. That's all.
不，謝了。那就夠了。

Dialogue 2

A : Come in. I'm glad to see you.
請進，我很高興見到你。

B : Thank you. It was nice of you to invite me to dinner.
謝謝你。你眞好，請我來晚餐。

A : Let me take your coat. Go on into the living room.
讓我來拿你的外套。到客廳去吧。

B : Dinner smells good.
晚餐好香。

A : Thanks. It'll be ready soon. Can I get you something
to drink?

謝謝。馬上就好了。要我給你拿些喝的嗎?

B : Yes. A glass of orange juice, please.

好的,請給我一杯柳橙汁。

Dialogue 3

A : What are you drinking?

你在喝什麼?

B : A coke.

可口可樂。

A : Can I get you another one?

我再給你一杯好嗎?

B : Yes, thank you.

好的,謝謝你。

A : How about something to eat?

吃點東西如何?

B : I'd like some popcorn.

我想要些爆米花。

〔舉一反三〕

A : Can I get you something to drink?

要我拿些喝的給你嗎?

B : Yes. I'd like some water.

好的,我想要一些水。

A : Can I get you something to eat?

我能給你拿些吃的嗎?

B : No, thank you, but I would like another drink.

不了,謝謝你,但是我想再喝一杯飲料。

A : I'm going to get another drink. Do you want anything?

我要再去拿一杯飲料，你要些什麼嗎？

B : Yes. I'll have another coke.

好，我要再喝一杯可口可樂。

A : Can I get you anything?

我能給你拿些什麼嗎？

B : Yes. I'd like a Scotch on the rocks, please.

好的，請給我一杯威士忌加冰塊。

A : Can I get anything for you?

我能替你拿些什麼嗎？

B : No, I'm fine. Thank you.

不了，我很好，謝謝你。

【註釋】

Have a seat.＝**Be seated.**＝**Sit down.** 坐下。

living room 起居室；客廳

smell 〔smɛl〕 *vi.* 發出氣味；發出香味或臭味

popcorn 〔'pɑpˌkɔrn〕 *n.* 爆米花

Scotch 〔skɑtʃ〕 *n.* 蘇格蘭威士忌酒

on the rocks （威士忌等）加冰塊

54. *Your guess is as good as mine.*

Dialogue 1

A : Say, Joe, when will we get a pay raise?
喂，喬，我們何時會加薪？

B : Your guess is as good as mine. I have no idea.
你想的跟我一樣。我沒概念。

A : When did you get your last raise?
你上回加薪是什麼時候？

B : Last October. I only hope I can keep this job.
去年十月。我只希望我能保住這份工作。

A : What do you mean?
你的意思是？

B : It seems that everybody's out of work because of the economy.
由於經濟的緣故，好像人人都在失業。

Dialogue 2

A : How many people showed up at the baseball game last night?
昨天晚上的棒球賽有多少人在場？

B : Why? 幹嘛？

A : If we can guess the right figure we can win a trip to Vegas.
如果我們能猜出正確的數字，我們就可以贏得免費到維加斯旅遊一趟。

B : There were so many people. I don't know what to say. Your guess is as good as mine.
有那麼多的人，我不知道有多少。你的猜測就跟我的一樣。

A : I know it's a long shot, but I'll say 7,000.

我知道這個很難猜，但是我會說有七千個。

B : I'll go along with that. 我同意那數目。

Dialogue 3

A : Which college do you think is better--Harvard or Yale?

哪一所大學你覺得比較好——哈佛或是耶魯？

B : I don't know. I've never given it much thought.

我不知道。我從未認眞地考慮過。

A : I'd like to go to college but I'm not sure which one is better. Do you know ?

我想上大學，但我不能確定哪一所比較好。你知道嗎？

B : Not really. When it comes to something like this, your guess is as good as mine.

並不眞的知道。當遇到這種事的時候，你想的跟我想的是一樣的。

A : I think I'll have to visit the two schools and see what they're offering.

我想我將必須去拜訪這兩所學校，同時看看他們提供些什麼課程。

B : Sounds like a very good idea.

像是個很好的主意。

〔舉一反三〕

A : Do you know who's getting the Oscar this year ?

你知道誰會得到今年的奧斯卡金像獎？

B : Your guess is as good as mine.

你想的跟我想的一樣。

A : What's the score ? 分數多少？

B : Your guess is as good as mine.

你猜的跟我猜的一樣。

A：Do you think the Dragons will beat the OB Bears?
你認爲龍隊會打敗 OB 熊隊嗎？

B：Beats me. 難倒我了。

A：Do you think he'll pass the test this time?
你認爲這回他會通過考試嗎？

B：God only knows. 天才會知道。

A：What are his chances of becoming a lawyer?
他成爲一個律師的機會有多少？

B：You know as much as I do.
你知道的跟我一樣多。

《 背景説明 》

別人問我們，我們不知道或不肯定時，通常會回答：I don't know. 還有許多説法，也是應該學會的，以免談話時太死板了。

Your guess is as good as mine. 「你想的跟我一樣。」可表示不知道或不確定。類似的用法還有 You know as much as I do.

Beats me. 「難倒我了。」 ***God only knows.*** 「天才會知道。」則是較活潑的口語用法。

【註釋】

pay〔pe〕*n.* 薪水　　raise〔rez〕*n.*（薪資等的）提高；加薪

as good as 跟～一樣　　***out of work*** 失業

show up 出現；在場　　figure〔'fɪgjɚ , 'fɪgɚ〕*n.* 數字

long shot 成功機會甚少的打賭　　***go along with*** 贊成

thought〔θɔt〕*n.* 考慮；關注　　Oscar〔'ɔskɚ , 'ɑskɚ〕*n.* 奧斯卡金像獎

score〔skor , skɔr〕*n.*（競賽的）得分；比數

Beats me. 難倒我了；我不知道。

55. I'm easy to please.

Dialogue 1

A : What kind of food would you like to have, Chinese or Italian?
你喜歡吃什麼樣的菜，中國菜或義大利菜？

B : Whatever. I'm easy to please.
什麼都可以。我很隨和。

A : Shall we have Chinese food then?
那麼我們吃中國菜囉？

B : Fine with me. 我沒關係。

A : Would you like to try sweet and sour pork?
你要不要嚐嚐糖醋肉？

B : Doesn't matter. I'm not hard to please.
無所謂。我不是很挑剔的。

Dialogue 2

A : That chicken looks delicious.
那隻雞看起來很可口。

B : It is. How's your steak?
它是的。你的牛排如何？

A : It's Okay. 還好。

B : It looks burnt.
它好像燒焦了。

A : It is, but it's all right.
是啊，但是沒關係。

B : You're certainly easy to please. I would've sent it back. 你的確很隨和。是我的話，就把它退回去了。

Dialogue 3

A : Did that customer send his steak back?
那位顧客退回他的牛排嗎？

B : Yes. He said it was too rare.
是的。他說太生了。

A : He's very hard to please.
他眞是難以取悅。

B : I guess now it'll be too well-done.
我猜現在它會太熟了。

A : Probably.
很可能。

B : Why don't you wait on him next time?
何不下次你去伺候他？

〔舉一反三〕

A : What do you want for your birthday?
你生日要什麼禮物？

B : Just give me money. I'm easy to please.
給我錢就好。我是很容易取悅的。

A : I don't know what to get her for her birthday.
我不知道要給她什麼生日禮物。

B : Is she hard to please?
她很難以取悅嗎？

A : My husband eats anything I cook.
我煮的東西我先生都吃。

B : I wish my husband was that easy to please.
我希望我先生那麼好伺候就好了。

A : Didn't he like his dinner?
　　他不喜歡他的晚餐嗎？
B : No. He's very fussy about what he eats.
　　不。他對吃的東西十分挑剔。

A : Did your boss like your proposal?
　　你的老板喜歡你的建議嗎？
B : No, he's difficult to please. I have to redo it.
　　不喜歡，他很難以取悅。我必須重做。

《背景説明》

　　I'm easy to please.「我很隨和。」表示對別人的選擇或決定沒有意見，可以用在各種情況；若表示「難以取悅」，則是 *He is hard* (*or difficult*) *to please.*

　　類似的用法還有 *He is picky about food.*「他對吃的很挑剔。」*He is fussy about food.*「他對吃的很挑剔。」

　　因此，別人問你：Shall we go to a movie or a play? 如果你沒意見，就可以説：It doesn't matter. I'm easy to please.

【註釋】

whatever (hwɑt'ɛvɚ) *pron.* 不論什麼；任何
sweet and sour pork 糖醋豬肉
delicious (dɪ'lɪʃəs) *adj.* 美味的　　steak (stek) *n.* 牛排
burnt (bɜnt) *adj.* 燒焦的　　rare (rɛr) *adj.* 未完全煮熟的
well-done ('wɛl'dʌn) *adj.* (肉) 煮 (烤) 全熟的
wait on sb. 伺候某人
fussy ('fʌsɪ) *adj.* 愛挑剔的；難以取悅的
proposal (prə'pozl) *n.* 建議；提議　　redo (ri'du) *vt.* 再做；重做

56. *Enjoy your meal.*

Dialogue 1

A : The food looks delicious.
這些食物看起來很可口。

B : Yes, we have a new French chef.
是的，我們有位新的法國主廚。

A : I can really tell the difference.
我能真正地分辨不同處。

B : I've heard nothing but good things about his preparations.
對於他調製的食物，我沒聽過有不好的評語。

A : Please give the chef my compliments.
請代我向這位大廚致讚美之意。

B : I certainly will. Enjoy your meal.
我當然會的。慢慢享用吧。

Dialogue 2

A : I'd like a steak, please, rare.
我要一份牛排，五分熟。

B : Do you want a baked potato or French fries?
你要烤馬鈴薯或是炸薯條？

A : Baked, please. 烤的，謝謝。

B : Will there be anything else?
要不要其他的東西呢？

A : Yes, a small salad. 是的，一小份沙拉。

B : All right, sir. Enjoy your meal.
好的，先生。好好享用你的一餐吧。

Dialogue 3

A : We'd like a table by the window, please.
我們想要一張靠窗的桌子。

B : A table for two?
兩個人的桌子？

A : Yes.
是的。

B : Will this table be all right?
這張桌子好嗎？

A : This is fine, thank you.
很好，謝謝你。

B : The waitress will be with you in a minute. Enjoy your meal.
女侍一會兒就來。請慢享用。

〔舉一反三〕

A : Enjoy your meal, sir.
盡情享用你的大餐，先生。

B : Thank you. It looks delicious.
謝謝你。它看起來很可口。

A : May I have some steak sauce?
能不能給我些牛排的佐料？

B : Here you are. Enjoy your meal.
這就是。好好享用吧。

A : This table is perfect. Thank you.
這張桌子很好。謝謝你。

B : I'm glad you like it. I hope you enjoy dining with us.
我很高興你喜歡它。我希望你會喜歡與我們一同用餐。

A : I'd like a table in the corner, please.

我想要一張在角落的桌子。

B : Here you are. Enjoy your lunch, sir.

這兒就是。享受你的午餐,先生。

A : A table for four, please.

四個人的桌子一張,謝謝。

B : Here you are. I hope you enjoy your dinner.

這兒就是。我希望你們晚餐吃得高興。

【註釋】

chef〔ʃɛf〕*n.* 主廚

tell〔tɛl〕*vt.* 辨別;辨識

preparation〔͵prɛpə'reʃən〕*n.* 準備;(調製成之)食物

compliment〔'kɑmpləmənt〕*n.* 恭維;稱讚

meal〔mil〕*n.* 餐

French fries 薯條(= *French fried potatoes*)

steak sauce 用來加在牛排上之佐料

in the corner 在角落

57. Two coffees, please.

Dialogue 1

A : Are you being helped?
　　有人招呼過你嗎？

B : No, I'd like to order two coffees, please.
　　沒有，我要叫兩杯咖啡。

A : Cream or sugar?
　　加奶精或加糖？

B : Just cream, please.
　　加奶精就好。

A : Would you like anything else?
　　你要不要其他的東西呢？

B : No, that's all.
　　不了，這樣就夠了。

Dialogue 2

A : What would you like, sir?
　　你想要些什麼？先生。

B : I'd like a coke and two coffees, please.
　　我要一杯可樂和兩杯咖啡。

A : Do you want cream or sugar with your coffee?
　　你的咖啡加奶精或加糖？

B : No, just black.
　　不要，什麼都不加。

A : Here or to go?
　　在這兒喝或帶走？

B : Here, please. 在這兒喝。

Dialogue 3

A : I would like to order two hamburgers.
　　我要點兩份漢堡。

B : What do you want on them?
　　你上面要加些什麼？

A : Everything but hold the onions.
　　除了洋蔥都要。

B : Anything else?
　　其他還點些什麼嗎？

A : Yes, two large cokes to go with it.
　　是的，兩份大杯可口可樂帶走。

B : All right, ma'am. Will that be all?
　　好的，女士。就這些嗎？

〔舉一反三〕

A : May I take your order?
　　您要點菜了嗎？

B : Yes. Two coffees, please.
　　是的，兩杯咖啡，謝謝。

A : A table for four, please.
　　四個人的桌子一張，謝謝。

B : Would you like to be near the orchestra?
　　你們要不要靠近樂隊的？

A : I'd like two boxes of popcorn and two cokes, please.
　　我要兩盒爆米花和兩杯可口可樂，謝謝。

B : Do you want a large size?
　　你要大的嗎？

A : Let's sit together.
　　我們坐在一塊兒吧。

B : O.K. I see two seats over there.
　　好的，我看到在那裏有兩個位子。

A : Did you order three cups of coffee?
　　你點了三杯咖啡嗎？

B : No, I only ordered two.
　　不，我只點了兩杯。

【註釋】

cream〔krim〕n. 乳脂；加在咖啡裏的奶精（ coffee-mate 奶精）

black 指不加牛奶、乳脂（甚或糖）的咖啡

hamburger〔'hæmbɝɡɚ〕n. 漢堡

onion〔'ʌnjən〕n. 洋蔥

ma'am〔mæm, mɑm〕= madam〔'mædəm〕n. 女士；夫人（對女子之尊稱）

orchestra〔'ɔrkɪstrə〕n. 管弦樂隊

large size 大號的

coke 可口可樂簡稱。　cola 可樂

58. *Would you like a refill?*

Dialogue 1

A : Sir, would you like a refill?
先生，你要不要再加滿？

B : No, thank you. I don't have enough money for more coffee.
不，謝謝你。我沒有足夠的錢再多喝咖啡。

A : We give refills at no extra charge. Don't worry.
我們再加滿不另外加錢。別擔心。

B : I think I'll have another cup.
我想我要再來一杯。

A : Here you are.
喏，這便是。

B : Thank you.
謝謝你。

Dialogue 2

A : Excuse me, Miss. I'd like a refill on my coffee, please.
對不起，小姐。我想再要一杯咖啡，謝謝。

B : Certainly.
當然可以。

A : My wife would like about a half a cup more, too.
我太太也想再要半杯。

B : If you need anything else, just let me know.
如果你需要其他東西，儘管告訴我。

A : Thanks. 謝謝。

B : Anytime. 隨時服務。

Dialogue 3

A : May I help you?
我能幫忙你嗎？

B : I need a refill for my ball point pen.
我的原子筆需要換筆芯。

A : What kind of pen do you have?
你的筆是哪一種？

B : It's a SKB.
它是枝「SKB」。

A : Let's see it. What color do you want?
讓我們瞧瞧。你要什麼顏色？

B : I'd like a light blue, if you have it.
如果有你的話，我要枝淺藍色的。

〔舉一反三〕

A : Would you like a refill?
你要不要再加滿？

B : Yes, please.
好的，謝謝。

A : Would you care for another cup of coffee, sir?
你要不要再來一杯咖啡？先生。

B : Yes, a refill please.
好的，請再加滿。

A : Excuse me, but I'd like a warm up, please.
對不起，但是我要一杯熱的，謝謝。

B : One refill coming right up.
馬上就來加滿。

A : I need a refill for my pen.
　　我的鋼筆需要加墨水。

B : Certainly. I'd be happy to help you.
　　當然可以，我很樂意幫助你。

A : I'd like to get this prescription refilled.
　　我想照這藥方再配一付藥。

B : All right. It will be ready in about fifteen minutes.
　　好的，大概十五分鐘就會好。

《背景説明》

　　Would you like a refill?「你要不要再加滿？」通常用於喝飲料等的時候，是主人或服務生詢問的話。如果還要，就説：***Yes, please.*** 或 ***Yes, a refill please.*** 也可用於其他場合，如換原子筆的筆芯也可説：***I'd like a refill*** for my ball point pen.

【註釋】

refill ('ri,fɪl) *n.* 再加滿；續杯；用以填補之物〔ri'fɪl〕*vt.* 再加滿；補充
extra charge 額外的費用；追加費用
ball point pen 原子筆
SKB 原子筆的廠牌名
light blue 淺藍色
care for 想要；喜歡（主要用於否定句、疑問句、條件子句）
warm up *n.* 加熱的東西　*v.* 重新加熱
prescription (prɪ'skrɪpʃən) *n.* 藥方；規定
fill a prescription 照藥方配藥

59. Can I have the check, please?

Dialogue 1

A : That was really a delicious meal, wasn't it?
那眞是可口美味的一餐，不是嗎？

B : It sure was. I always enjoy coming here.
的確是，我總是喜歡來這兒。

A : Ready to go?
準備走了吧？

B : Yes, let's go. Miss, can I have the check, please?
好的，咱們走。小姐，能給我帳單嗎？

A : Let me get that.
讓我來付。

B : No, you picked it up the last time. It's my turn.
不成，上次你付的，這回輪到我了。

Dialogue 2

A : It's been fun having lunch with you today.
今天跟你一塊兒吃午餐眞愉快。

B : That goes for me, too. Let's do it more often.
我也有同樣的感覺。讓我們更常一塊兒吃午飯吧。

A : Well, we'd better get back to work. Waitress, may we have our checks, please?
嗯，我們最好回去工作了。女侍，請給我們帳單好嗎？

B : Do you want separate checks?
你們要分開付帳嗎？

A : Yes, please.
　　是的。

B : O.K. Just a moment.
　　好。等一下。

Dialogue 3

A : Since this is our first time here, I wonder how we take care of the tab.
　　既然這是我們第一次來這兒，我想知道我們如何付帳。

B : We can ask the waiter when he returns.
　　侍者回來時我們可以問他。

A : Excuse me, do we pay you or the cashier?
　　對不起，請問我們付錢給你或付給櫃台？

B : You pay me and I'll take care of it for you, sir.
　　你付給我，我會替你處理。

A : We are ready to leave now. May we have the tab?
　　我們現在準備要走了。可以給我們帳單嗎？

B : Yes, sir. I'll have it ready in a moment.
　　好的，先生，我很快就會準備好。

〔舉一反三〕

A : May I have the check, please?
　　請給我帳單好嗎？

B : Yes, sir.
　　好的，先生。

A : I would like the tab, please.
　　請給我帳單。

B : All right, sir.
　　好的，先生。

A : Can I have the bill, please?
　　請給我帳單好嗎？
B : One moment, ma'am.
　　等一會兒，女士。

A : Please put this on my tab.
　　請把這個加在我的帳單上。
B : Certainly, we'll take care of it for you.
　　當然可以，我們會為您處理。

A : Separate checks, please.
　　請分開結帳。
B : Just a moment, Miss.
　　請等一會兒，小姐。

【註釋】

check〔tʃɛk〕*n.* 帳單；支票
pick up（俗語）替人付帳
It's my turn. 輪到我了；該我了。
separate〔'sɛpərɪt〕*adj.* 分開的；各別的
wonder〔'wʌndɚ〕*vt.* 想知道
take care of 處理
tab〔tæb〕*n.* 帳單；費用
cashier〔kæ'ʃɪr〕*n.* 出納員（指在櫃台收費者）
in a moment 立刻；馬上
bill〔bɪl〕*n.* 帳單　　***put on*** 加上

60. So so.

Dialogue 1

A : How did the party turn out?
這個宴會結果如何?

B : It was all right, I guess.
還可以,我想。

A : What do you mean?
你的意思是?

B : Not very many people showed up.
沒有很多人到場。

A : How was the food?
食物怎麼樣?

B : So so. 普通。

Dialogue 2

A : When did you get back from your vacation?
你何時休假回來的?

B : Last night.
昨晚。

A : How was the fishing?
釣魚釣得怎樣?

B : So so. The water was too rough.
平平。風浪太大了。

A : Were you able to catch anything?
你能釣到些什麼嗎?

B : Yes, but it could have been a lot better.
可以的,但是本來可以更好的。

Dialogue 3

A : Why are you so angry?
　　你爲何如此生氣？

B : My application was rejected.
　　我的申請被駁回了。

A : Why was it rejected?
　　爲什麼被駁回呢？

B : I was given the wrong form.
　　他們給錯表格了。

A : How did that happen?
　　怎麼會那樣呢？

B : Oh, that so-and-so Mr. Yi got the forms mixed up.
　　噢，那位可惡的易先生把表格搞混了。

〔舉一反三〕

A : Your steak looks good. How does it taste?
　　你的牛排看起來很好，嚐起來如何？

B : Just so so. It's a little tough.
　　僅僅普通罷了。有點兒老。

A : How did the meeting go?
　　會開得怎樣？

B : So so. Half the people were absent.
　　沒什麼。一半的人缺席。

A : How was the movie?
　　這部電影如何？

B : So so. I liked the book better.
　　平平。我比較喜歡原書。

A : How was your meal at that new restaurant?
你在那家新餐廳吃的如何？

B : It was O.K., nothing special.
尚可，沒什麼特別的。

A : Joe is a tough boss.
喬是個難侍候的老板。

B : İ agree. He's a real so-and-so to work for.
我同意。他真是個令人討厭的老板。

《背景說明》

So so. 類似中文的「如此而已」，因此譯成「馬馬虎虎；平平」，可以用來形容人或事物，表示沒有什麼特別好或特別差。

so-and-so 通常指「某某」，所以 Mr. so-and-so 就是「某某先生」，也可用於人或事物。

so-and-so 的另一個意思，則是一種詛咒語，相當於「該死的（人、事物）」，例如：That *so-and-so* didn't come to work again. 「那個討厭的傢伙又沒來上班。」

【註釋】

So so. 馬馬虎虎；差強人意；不好不壞。

turn out 結果；竟然　*show up* 出現；到場

get back 回來　rough〔rʌf〕*adj.* 波濤洶湧的

application〔͵æplə'keʃən〕*n.* 申請；應用

reject〔rɪ'dʒɛkt〕*vt.* 拒絕；不接受

so-and-so〔'soən͵so〕*adj.* 詛咒語（= *damned*）該死的

　n. 討厭的傢伙；可惡的傢伙；某人；某事物

mix up 使混亂；使糊塗

tough〔tʌf〕*adj.* 堅韌的；粗暴的；難侍候的　　taste〔test〕*vi.,vi.* 品嚐

61. It's Greek to me.

Dialogue 1

A : Does he make any sense to you?
他說的話你懂嗎？

B : No. It's Greek to me.
不，它對我而言好像是希臘文。

A : No. He's speaking Chinese.
不，他說的是中文。

B : I know he's speaking Chinese. I said, I didn't understand what he meant.
我知道他是在說中文。我的意思是我不了解他在說什麼。

A : Now I see. 現在我明白了。

B : I wish I could understand the Chinese language.
我希望我能懂得中文。

Dialogue 2

A : Tom, could you help me with this?
湯姆，你能幫我看這個嗎？

B : Sure. What's the problem?
當然。有什麼問題呢？

A : Can you read this?
你能解說這個嗎？

B : No, I can't. What language is this?
不，我不能。這是什麼語言？

A : I think it's Japanese. 我想它是日文。

B : Well, it's Greek to me.
噢，我一點兒也不懂日文。

Dialogue 3

A : What's wrong?
怎麼了？

B : I'm having a lot of trouble with these directions.
我為這些指示所苦。

A : Let me see them. Maybe I can help.
讓我瞧瞧，也許我能幫得上忙。

B : This is the part I don't understand.
這就是我不懂的部分。

A : Hmm. I'm afraid it's Greek to me.
嗯。我恐怕也不懂。

B : Thank you, anyway.
不管怎樣，謝謝你。

〔舉一反三〕

A : I can't understand this map.
我不能了解這張地圖。

B : Me, either. It's Greek to me.
我也是，也不懂。

A : Do you understand these directions?
你了解這些指示嗎？

B : No. They're Greek to me.
不，它們是我無法了解的。

A : Can you read this?
這個你看得懂嗎？

B : No. It's Greek to me.
不，我不能了解。

A : What was he saying?

他說些什麼?

B : I don't know. I couldn't understand what he was talking about.

我不知道。我不能了解他在說些什麼。

A : Can you understand this sentence?

你能了解這個句子嗎?

B : No, I can't.

不,我不能。

―――

【註釋】

make sense 能夠理解;有道理
It's Greek to me. 這我完全不懂。
direction 〔 dəˈrɛkʃən, daɪˈrɛkʃən 〕 *n.* 說明;指示
anyway 〔ˈɛnɪˌwe 〕 *adv.* 無論如何

I can't understand this map.

Me, either. It's Greek to me.

62. Let's give him a big hand.

Dialogue 1

A : The performance given by this group was sensational.
這一團表演得眞令人激動。

B : Let's give them a big hand.
讓我們給他們熱烈鼓掌。

A : They've had to work long hours to pull this off so well.
他們一定練了很久才能表演得這麼好。

B : Oh, there's no doubt about it.
喔，那是毫無疑問的。

A : Did you know they're from our hometown?
你知道他們是從我們家鄉來的嗎？

B : No, I didn't know that.
不，我不知道。

Dialogue 2

A : How was the dinner they had for John?
他們爲約翰安排的晚餐如何？

B : It was lovely. 很愉快。

A : Was the food good? 食物好嗎？

B : It was excellent. The restaurant did a good job.
太好了。這餐廳做得很好。

A : How was John's speech?
約翰的演說如何？

B : Very good. They gave him a big hand.
非常好。他們給他熱烈鼓掌。

Dialogue 3

A : How was the dance recital?
　　那場舞蹈表演會如何？

B : Great! The children did a beautiful job.
　　棒極了！孩子們表演得十分漂亮。

A : I'll bet they were cute.
　　我相信他們很可愛。

B : Oh, they were. Their costumes were darling.
　　噢，他們是。他們服裝真可愛。

A : Did Jane dance well?
　　珍跳得好嗎？

B : She was excellent. She got a standing ovation.
　　她好極了。她得到的鼓掌喝采持久不歇。

〔舉一反三〕

A : How was the fashion show?
　　那場服裝發表會如何？

B : Great! They gave the designer a big hand.
　　太好了！他們給設計者熱烈鼓掌。

A : He should get a big hand.
　　他應該得到熱烈的鼓掌。

B : Right! He's an excellent singer.
　　沒錯！他是個傑出的歌手。

A : The audience must like her. She's really getting a big hand.
　　觀眾一定很喜歡她。她正在接受熱烈鼓掌。

B : She's very popular.
　　她非常受歡迎。

A : Was the President's speech good?

　　總統的演講精釆嗎？

B : Yes. He received a standing ovation.

　　是的，他受到起立鼓掌。

A : Who are they clapping for?

　　他們在為誰鼓掌？

B : Paul. He's been playing the piano.

　　保羅。他在彈鋼琴。

【註釋】

performance〔pəˈfɔrməns〕*n.* 表演；演出
sensational〔sɛnˈseʃənḷ〕*adj.* 令人激動的；聳人聽聞的
hand〔hænd〕*n.* 拍手喝釆
pull off （俗語）圓滿完成（困難的事）
hometown〔ˈhomˈtaʊn〕*n.* 家鄉
excellent〔ˈɛksḷənt〕*adj.* 最好的；特優的
recital〔rɪˈsaɪtḷ〕*n.* 表演會
cute〔kjut〕*adj.* 美麗可愛逗人喜歡的；伶俐的
costume〔ˈkɑstjum〕*n.* 服裝；戲服
darling〔ˈdɑrlɪŋ〕*adj.* 可愛的
standing〔ˈstændɪŋ〕*adj.* 起立的；持續的
ovation〔oˈveʃən〕*n.* 熱烈的喝釆鼓掌
standing ovation 起立鼓掌；持久鼓掌喝釆
clap〔klæp〕*vi.* 鼓掌

63. As far as I'm concerned.

Dialogue 1

A : Say, Ron. Long time no see. How have you been?
嘿，朗。好久不見了。你最近怎樣？

B : Pretty busy. How have you been?
相當忙。你近況如何呢？

A : No complaints. Let's get together one of these days.
沒什麼不好。哪天咱們聚聚。

B : Sounds good. Would this Friday evening be all right with you?
好像不錯。這禮拜五晚上可以嗎？

A : As far as I'm concerned, that's fine.
我這方面沒問題。

B : Good. I'll see you then.
好，到時候見。

Dialogue 2

A : Isn't that dog beautiful!
那隻狗眞漂亮！

B : He sure is. 牠的確是。

A : Do you think I could ever get a dog?
你認爲我能不能養一隻狗？

B : As far as I'm concerned, you can have one now.
對我來說，你現在就能養一隻。

A : Really? 眞的嗎？

B : Sure. Let's find out how much that one costs.
當然。咱們去看看那一隻要花多少錢。

Dialogue 3

A : That sun really feels good.
那太陽令人感覺舒服。

B : Let's go for a swim!
咱們去游泳吧！

A : No, I don't want to, but you go on ahead.
不，我不想去，但是你儘管去。

B : Why don't you want to swim?
你爲何不去游泳？

A : As far as I'm concerned, that water is too cold.
對我來說，水太冷了。

B : No, it's not. It's perfect!
不，不會的。它正好！

〔舉一反三〕

A : Do you think Nick is honest?
你認爲尼克誠實嗎？

B : As far as I'm concerned, he is.
對我來說，他是的。

A : As far as I'm concerned, this meeting is a waste of time.
對我來說，這個會議只是在浪費時間。

B : Do you want to leave?
你要離開嗎？

A : Who's going to win the election?
誰將贏得選舉？

B : As far as I'm concerned, neither candidate is any good. 對我來講，沒有一個候選人是好的。

A : Roger wants to buy a new motorcycle.
　　羅傑想要買輛新摩托車。

B : As far as I'm concerned, he can.
　　就我所知，他可以。

A : Which of these dresses do you like best?
　　這些衣服裏你最喜歡哪一件？

B : As far as I'm concerned, they're the same.
　　對我來說，它們都一樣。

【註釋】

Long time no see. 好久不見。

pretty〔'prɪtɪ〕*adv.* 相當地；十分　*adj.* 漂亮的

complaint〔kəm'plent〕*n.* 訴苦；抱怨

as far as sb. is concerned 就某人而言；據某人所知；至於某人

perfect〔'pɜfɪkt〕*adj.* 理想的；完美的

waste〔west〕*n.* 浪費

a waste of time 白費時間

election〔ɪ'lɛkʃən〕*n.* 選舉

candidate〔'kændə,det , 'kændədɪt〕*n.* 候選人

motorcycle〔'motə,saɪkl̩〕*n.* 摩托車

64. I got here at five sharp.

Dialogue 1

A : I'm sorry I'm late. The traffic was terrible.
我很抱歉我遲到了。交通太糟糕了。

B : It's all right. Take your time.
沒關係的。你慢慢來。

A : What time did you get here?
你什麼時候到這兒的？

B : I got here at five sharp.
我五點正到這兒。

A : Well, shall we order something to drink?
噢，我們要不要點些喝的？

B : Fine. Whatever you say. 好啊。隨便你。

Dialogue 2

A : Oh, oh. I left my wallet on the table in the coffee shop.
噢，噢。我把我的皮包留在咖啡店的桌子上了。

B : You'd better go back and get it right away.
你最好立刻趕回去拿。

A : I'll be late to the meeting.
我會趕不上開會。

B : What time does it start? 它什麼時候開始？

A : It's supposed to start at two sharp.
應該是兩點正開始。

B : You'd better hurry. I'll wait for you in the lobby.
你最好快點。我在大廳等你。

Dialogue 3

A : Isn't Keith here yet? I wanted to get an early start.
　　凱茲還沒來嗎？我想早點開始。

B : What time did you tell him to meet us?
　　你告訴他什麼時候跟我們碰面？

A : I told him to be here at six on the dot.
　　我告訴他六點正來這兒。

B : Well, it's six-fifteen now. What do you want to do?
　　噢，現在六點十五分了。你要怎麼辦？

A : I'd like to go off and leave him.
　　我要走了，不管他了。

B : Let's wait a few more minutes.
　　我們再多等幾分鐘吧。

〔舉一反三〕

A : What time did the meeting start?
　　這會議什麼時候開始的？

B : It started at five sharp.
　　五點正開始。

A : Do you have to leave so early?
　　你必須這麼早離開嗎？

B : Yes. I promised to be home by ten sharp.
　　是的。我答應要在十點正前回家。

A : Are we going to the concert?
　　我們要去聽音樂會嗎？

B : No, it's too late. They close the doors at exactly seven o'clock.
　　不，太遲了。他們在七點正就關門了。

A : I see Tom's here already.

　　我看到湯姆已經來這兒了。

B : He's always on time.

　　他總是準時的。

A : How long have you been waiting?

　　你已經等多久了？

B : I got here right at five on the dot.

　　我五點正來這兒的。

【註釋】

Take your time. 慢慢來；不要急。

sharp 〔ʃɑrp〕 *adv.* 準；正；整

wallet 〔'wɑlɪt〕 *n.* 皮包；皮夾

be supposed to 應該

lobby 〔'lɑbɪ〕 *n.* 大廳；休息室

on the dot 準時

dot 〔dɑt〕 *n.* 點

by ten sharp 在十點正以前；不遲於十點正

concert 〔'kɑnsɝt〕 *n.* 音樂會

on time 準時　　*in time* 及時

65. I'm all mixed up.

Dialogue 1

A : Where were you yesterday?
你昨天去哪兒了？

B : Yesterday? I was at home. Why?
昨天？我在家啊。幹嘛？

A : You were supposed to meet me for lunch.
你應該跟我碰面吃午餐的。

B : No. Our date is for tomorrow, Thursday.
不。我們的約會是在明天，星期四。

A : No, it was yesterday, Tuesday.
不，是昨天，星期二。

B : Oh, you're right. I'm all mixed up on the days.
噢，你是對的。這些日子我全搞混了。

Dialogue 2

A : What are you looking for?
你在找些什麼？

B : I'm trying to figure out which one is which. I've mixed up my contact lenses.
我正試著找出哪一個是哪個。我把我的隱形眼鏡弄混了。

A : I understand. I have the same problem once in a while.
我了解。有時我也有同樣的難題。

B : Do you wear contact lenses, too?
你也戴隱形眼鏡嗎？

A : Yes I do. I find them more convenient than glasses.
　　　是的，我戴。我發現它們比眼鏡方便。

B : I agree.
　　　我同意。

Dialogue 3

A : Aren't you Yung-ho Yi?
　　　你不是易揚侯嗎？

B : No. My name is John Kao.
　　　不，我是高約翰。

A : You certainly look familiar. Did I meet you last week?
　　　你看起來真的很面熟。我上禮拜遇見過你嗎？

B : No. You must have me mixed up with someone else.
　　　沒有。你一定把我跟另一個人搞錯了。

A : I'm sorry I bothered you.
　　　我很抱歉打擾你了。

B : That's all right.
　　　沒關係。

〔舉一反三〕

A : Tom got his appointments all mixed up today.
　　　湯姆今天把他的約會都弄亂了。

B : Is that why he's late?
　　　那就是他遲到的原因嗎？

A : The train left ten minutes ago.
　　　這班火車十分鐘前離開。

B : Oh! I must have gotten the schedule mixed up.
　　　噢！我一定是把時間表弄混了。

A： I'm Joe, he's Jack.
　　我是喬，他是傑克。

B： I'm sorry. I got your names mixed up.
　　我很抱歉。我把你們的名字弄混了。

A： Is he speaking Chinese?
　　他正在講中文嗎？

B： No, Japanese. You're confusing the languages.
　　不，日文。你把這些語言搞混了。

A： Is this the track where I catch the train to Kaohsiung?
　　這就是那條我搭火車去高雄的鐵路嗎？

B： No. You're confused. It's that track.
　　不，你弄錯了，是那條鐵路。

《背景說明》

　　I'm all mixed up.「我搞混了。」意思與 *I'm confused.* 相近，可以用於各類情況。如：*The foreigner is all mixed up* on our names.「那個外國人把我們名字全搞混了。」*I'm mixed up* on the time.「我把時間搞錯了。」*I'm all mixed up* about the people.「我把人都搞混了。」

【註釋】

mix up 使混亂；使糊塗　　*figure out* 理解
contact lenses 隱形眼鏡
convenient〔kən'vinjənt〕*adj.* 方便的；舒適的
familiar〔fə'mɪljə〕*adj.* 熟悉的　　bother〔'bɑðə〕*vt.* 煩擾；困擾
appointment〔ə'pɔɪntmənt〕*n.* 約會　　schedule〔'skɛdʒul〕*n.* 時間表
confuse〔kən'fjuz〕*vt.* 使混亂　　track〔træk〕*n.* 鐵路的路線；軌道

66. *I've had enough*.

Dialogue 1

A : Would you like some more fish?
　　你要不要再來些魚？

B : No, thanks. I've had enough.
　　不了，謝謝。我已經吃夠了。

A : How about a little more rice?
　　再來一點飯如何？

B : I'm really full. Thanks.
　　我真的飽了。謝謝。

A : I hope you enjoy the food.
　　我希望你喜歡這食物。

B : I liked it very much.
　　我非常喜歡它。

Dialogue 2

A : I've had enough of him.
　　我已經受夠他了。

B : What's the matter? 怎麼回事？

A : This is the third time he's made the same mistake.
　　這已經是他第三次犯同樣的錯誤。

B : Did you tell him not to do it?
　　你有沒有告訴他不要這樣做？

A : Yes, but he never listens.
　　有啊，但是他從來都不聽。

B : Maybe you should have a serious talk with him.
　　也許你該認真地跟他談談。

Dialogue 3

A : How about another game of tennis?
再打一局網球如何？

B : Not me. I've had enough for one day.
不要找我。我這一天已經打夠了。

A : Come on. I'll go easy on you.
別這樣，來啦！我會輕鬆地跟你打。

B : No, two sets are all I can take.
不成，我只能打兩局。

A : Let's go get something to drink then.
那麼咱們去喝點東西。

B : O.K. I'll treat.
好，我請客。

〔舉一反三〕

A : Would you like some more coffee?
你要不要再來點咖啡？

B : No, thank you. I've had enough.
不，謝謝你。我已經喝夠了。

A : How about another piece of pie?
再來塊派如何？

B : No, I've had plenty, thanks.
不了，我已經吃很多了，謝謝。

A : Let's take a walk along the beach.
咱們沿著海灘散散步吧。

B : No. I've had enough exercise for one day.
不。我一天的運動已經夠了。

A : I'm full!
　　我吃飽了！

B : Are you sure you wouldn't like some dessert?
　　你確定你不要些甜點嗎？

A : Jack, I dented the fender on the car.
　　傑克，我把車子的擋衝板弄凹了。

B : Oh, no! I've had enough problems already today.
　　噢，不！我今天已經有夠多的問題了。

┌─────────────────────────────┐
│ 　《背景說明》
│
│　　*I've had enough.*「我已經吃夠了。」和 *I'm full.*「我吃飽了。」
│ *I've had plenty.*「我已經吃很多了。」意思相同，都是表示 I can't
│ eat another bite.「我一口也吃不下了。」
│　　I've had enough. 的另外一個意思是「我受夠了。」等於 *I can't*
│ *stand (or take) it any more.* 如：*I've had enough* of his
│ drinking.「我再也無法忍受他喝酒了。」
└─────────────────────────────┘

【註釋】

rice〔raɪs〕*n.* 米；飯
enough〔ə'nʌf, ɪ'nʌf〕*n.* 足夠的量（數）
full〔fʊl〕*adj.* 吃飽的；（胸口）發脹的　　**I am full.** 我吃飽了。
have had enough of 受夠了；厭煩了
have a talk with ～ 與～會談
set 為網球的一局，包含五場（ five games ）。
treat〔trit〕*vt., vi.* 款待；請客　　plenty〔'plɛntɪ〕*n.* 充分；多
dent〔dɛnt〕*vt.* 弄成凹痕；使成缺口
fender〔'fɛndɚ〕*n.* 擋泥板；緩衝板（火車、汽車等車頭為緩和碰撞所裝的）

67. Let's get together one of these days.

Dialogue 1

A : Hi, Tony.
嗨，東尼。

B : Hi, Alice.
嗨，艾莉絲。

A : It's been a long time since we met.
從上次碰面到現在已經很久了。

B : It sure has.
真的是。

A : Let's get together one of these days.
咱們找一天聚聚。

B : That sounds great.
好像很好。

Dialogue 2

A : Jimmy? I hardly recognized you.
吉米？我幾乎認不出你。

B : Hi, Sue. I haven't seen you for a long time.
嗨，蘇。我很久沒有看到妳了。

A : Right. What have you been doing?
是的。你都在做些什麼？

B : Working as usual. How about you?
跟平常一樣工作。妳怎麼樣呢？

A : The same. We should get together one of these
days and talk.

老樣子。我們應該找一天聚聚聊一聊。

B : Sure. Give me a call.

當然。打電話給我。

Dialogue 3

A : I've enjoyed talking to you.

很高興跟你談話。

B : Same here. Let's get together again soon.

我也一樣。讓咱們儘快再聚聚。

A : Sure. I'd like you to meet my wife.

當然。我要你見見我太太。

B : Good idea. I'll give you a call.

好主意。我會打電話給你。

A : Maybe sometime next week.

也許下個禮拜。

B : Fine.

好的。

〔舉一反三〕

A : I enjoyed meeting you.

見到你真高興。

B : Let's get together one of these days.

咱們找哪天聚聚。

A : Let's get together again.

咱們再聚聚。

B : Good idea. I'll give you a call.

好主意。我會給你電話。

A : We should get together more often.
　　我們應該更常聚在一起。

B : Right. It's been fun talking to you.
　　是的。跟你談天很快樂。

A : When are we going to get together?
　　我們什麼時候聚一聚？

B : How about sometime next week?
　　下禮拜如何？

A : Nice talking to your.
　　跟你談天真好。

B : Give me a call sometime. We'll have lunch.
　　改天打個電話給我。我們一塊兒吃午餐。

【註釋】

one of these days 這幾天內；近日內；不久

recognize (ˈrɛkəgˌnaɪz) *vt.* 認識；認得

as usual 照常；照例

give *sb.* ***a call*** 打電話給某人

sometime (ˈsʌmˌtaɪm) *adv.* 改天；近日內；某時

68. *He's behind the times*.

Dialogue 1

A : Are you taking economics this summer?
今夏你選修經濟學了嗎？

B : Yes, I am. 是的，我是。

A : Who's your professor?
你的教授是誰？

B : Professor Johnson. He's behind the times.
強生教授。他落伍了。

A : Why do you say that?
你為何那樣說？

B : He's teaching the same thing he taught ten years ago.
他現在教的跟他十年前教的一樣。

Dialogue 2

A : Are you going to the dance on Friday?
你禮拜五要去跳舞嗎？

B : No. My father won't let me.
不。我父親不讓我去。

A : He's really strict, isn't he?
他的確很嚴厲，不是嗎？

B : Yes. He doesn't want me to date until I'm seventeen.
是的，他不准我十七歲以前約會。

A : He's really behind the times.
他真是趕不上時代。

B : He's just very old fashioned.
他只是很守舊。

Dialogue 3

A : You're not going to wear those pants, are you?
　　你不會要穿那些褲子吧，是不是？

B : What's wrong with them?
　　它們哪兒不對勁？

A : They're out of style.
　　它們不流行了。

B : Why do you say that?
　　你爲何那麼說？

A : No one wears flared pants anymore.
　　再也沒有人穿褲裙了。

B : Darn! They're my favorite pants.
　　眞可惡！它們是我最喜愛的褲子。

〔舉一反三〕

A : Look at the suit that guy is wearing.
　　看那傢伙穿的西裝。

B : He's really behind the times.
　　他眞的是跟不上時代。

A : That hair style went out in the fifties.
　　那種髮型在 50 年代就不流行了。

B : She's really behind the times.
　　她眞是落伍過時。

A : I don't like to shop in that store.
　　我不喜歡在那家店買東西。

B : I don't either. He doesn't keep up with the latest
styles.
　　我也不喜歡。它趕不上最新流行的款式。

A : My father says I have to be home by nine-thirty.
　　我父親說我必須在九點半以前回家。

B : Wow! He's really old fashioned.
　　哇！他真是老古板。

A : Can't I use these applications?
　　我不能用這些申請書嗎？

B : No. They're outdated. We have new ones.
　　不行的。它們是過時的，我們有新的。

=== 《背景説明》 ===

　　behind the times 就是「趕不上時代；落伍」，類似的用法還有 *outdated, out of style* 等。其用法如：The dictionary is *outdated*. 「那本字典已經落伍了。」These expressions are *outdated*. 「這些用法已經過時了。」I need a new coat. My old one is *out of style*. 「我需要買件新外套，舊的那件已經不流行了。」

　　注意另外一個片語 *behind time* 「遲到」（= *late* ）的形式接近，但意義相差很遠，time 加 S 表「時代；時期」，加冠詞 the。behind time 的 time 「時間」是抽象名詞，不加冠詞，也不可加 S。

【註釋】

take〔tek〕*vt.* 選擇　　　*behind the times* 落伍；趕不上時代
dance〔dæns〕*n.* 舞會　　strict〔strɪkt〕*adj.* 嚴格的；嚴厲的
old fashioned 守舊的；舊式的
pants〔pænts〕*n. pl.* 褲子（flared pants 褲裙）　　*out of style* 不流行
darn〔dɑrn〕*v.*（= *damn* ）咒罵（做為咒罵，發誓的驚歎詞）
suit〔sut, sɪut, sjut〕*n.*（衣服等的）一套；西裝　　*go out* 不流行；過時
shop〔ʃɑp〕*vi.* 購物　　*keep up with* 跟上（時代）；趕得上
outdated〔aut'detɪd〕*adj.* 過時的；老式的

69. *Do you take cream in your coffee?*

Dialogue 1

A : Would you like some coffee?
你要不要些咖啡？

B : Yes, please. 好的。

A : Do you take cream in your coffee?
你咖啡要加奶精嗎？

B : Yes, just a touch.
好的，只要一點。

A : How about sugar?
糖呢？

B : No, thanks. 不了，謝謝。

Dialogue 2

A : I'd like a cup of coffee, please.
我要一杯咖啡，謝謝。

B : Do you take cream in your coffee?
你咖啡要加奶精嗎？

A : No, but I'd like sugar. And make that to go, please.
不，但是我要加糖。而且要帶走的，謝謝。

B : Will that be all?
那就夠了嗎？

A : Yes, thank you.
是的，謝謝你。

B : That'll be fifty cents. 一共是五十分。

Dialogue 3

A : May I get you some coffee or tea?
　　我可以給你拿些茶或咖啡嗎?

B : Yes, some tea, please.
　　好，請給我些茶。

A : Do you like it strong or weak?
　　你要濃一點或淡一點?

B : Strong with lots of cream.
　　濃的，多加點奶精。

A : I've never heard of cream in tea.
　　我從沒聽過茶裏頭加奶精的。

B : Oh, that's an old custom that goes way back in my family.
　　噢，那是我家人長久以來的老習慣。

〔舉一反三〕

A : Do you take cream in your coffee?
　　你的咖啡加不加奶精?

B : Yes, please. Just a touch.
　　要的，謝謝。只要一點。

A : Would you care to have cream in your coffee?
　　你咖啡裏要不要加奶精?

B : Yes, heavy on the cream, please.
　　好的，請多加一點奶精。

A : Cream or sugar in your coffee, sir?
　　你的咖啡加奶精或糖，先生?

B : Sugar only, thank you.
　　只要糖，謝謝你。

A : How do you want your coffee?

　　你的咖啡要加什麼？

B : Cream and sugar, please.

　　請加奶精和糖。

A : Coffee to go, please.

　　咖啡外帶。

B : Anything in it?

　　加些什麼嗎？

【註釋】

a touch of ~ 少量的~

to go 外帶；（食物）買了可帶回去吃的（不在賣的店裏或攤子上吃）

cent〔sɛnt〕*n.* 分（一元的百分之一）

strong 濃　　weak 淡

custom〔'kʌstəm〕*n.* 習俗；慣例

go way back = *for a long time* 長久以來

heavy〔'hɛvɪ〕*adj.*（飲料）濃的

70. *I'll see you next Sunday*.

Dialogue 1

A : Hello, this is Mr. Smith speaking.
哈囉，我是史密斯先生。

B : Hi, this is Mac. Why didn't you show up last Sunday?
嗨，我是麥克。上星期天你為何沒有到？

A : What do you mean?
你的意思是？

B : You told me to meet you last Sunday, didn't you?
你叫我上星期天跟你碰面，不是嗎？

A : No, I said next Sunday, not this Sunday.
不，我說的是下星期天，不是這個星期天。

B : Oh, I guess I misunderstood you.
噢，我想我誤會你了。

Dialogue 2

A : Good morning, Tom. I'm calling to find out if you'll be able to work for me next Thursday.
早安，湯姆。我打電話給你是想知道你下星期四是否能替我工作。

B : Sure. Now, is that this Thursday or next Thursday?
當然。那麼，是這星期四或下星期四？

A : Next Thursday. 下星期四。

B : Let me check my schedule before I commit myself.
在我答應做這件工作前，讓我查查我的時間表。

A : All right. 好的。

B : Well, looks like I'm free so see you next Thursday.
嗯，我好像有空，下星期四見。

Dialogue 3

A : Would you like to come to dinner a week from
tomorrow?
你下個禮拜的明天來吃晚餐好嗎？

B : Let's see. That would be a week from Sunday, right?
咱們瞧瞧。那是下個禮拜天，對吧？

A : Yes, that's right.
是的，沒錯。

B : I believe I'd be able to make it.
我想我能來的。

A : Good. We'll be looking forward to seeing you then.
好的。我們期盼那時見到你。

B : Thanks for asking me.
謝謝邀請我。

〔舉一反三〕

A : Are you sure he said next Tuesday?
你確定他說下星期二嗎？

B : Yes, I'm sure it's one week from today.
是的，我確定是下禮拜的今天。

A : Let's get together this coming Friday evening.
咱們在這禮拜五晚上聚聚。

B : O.K. That sounds good to me.
好。好像不錯。

A : Can you work this coming Saturday?
這星期六你能來工作嗎？

B : You mean this Saturday?
你是指這個星期六？

A : I'll see you the day after tomorrow, all right?
後天見好嗎？

B : That's fine with me.
我沒問題。

A : Did you say the accident happened the day before yesterday?
你說這意外是前天發生的嗎？

B : Yes, that's what my friend told me.
是的，我朋友是那麼告訴我的。

《 背景說明 》

英文的 *next Sunday* 指「從明天起的第二個星期日」，如果要表示「緊接著的那個星期日」，則要說 *this Sunday* 或 *coming Sunday* 或 *this coming Sunday*。因此在約定日子的時候，必須說明清楚，以免誤解而記錯，最好能加上日期。

【註釋】

misunderstand (ˋmɪsʌndəˋstænd) *vt.* 誤會；誤解
commit oneself 承諾；承擔；使自己負責任或受約束
a week from tomorrow 下星期的明天
make it 達成某項的目標；成功
coming (ˋkʌmɪŋ) *adj.* 其次的 (= *next*)；將來的
the day after tomorrow 後天
accident (ˋæksədənt) *n.* 意外事件；偶發之事
the day before yesterday 前天

71. I'm pressed for time.

Dialogue 1

A : Bill, will you come over here and give me a hand with this problem?

比爾，你過來幫我解決這個問題好嗎？

B : Not now. Maybe later.

現在不行。也許晚一點。

A : Just give me a minute, will you?

只要一分鐘，好嗎？

B : No, sorry. I'm really pressed for time.

不行，抱歉。我真的時間緊迫。

A : Why?

為什麼？

B : Because I have to get this report finished in time for class.

因為我必須及時完成這份課堂上要用的報告。

Dialogue 2

A : Say, Bob. How about stopping by the house for a drink tonight?

嘿，鮑伯。今天晚上順道過來喝一杯如何？

B : I'd sure like to, but I'm quite pressed for time this evening.

我當然想，但是我今天晚上相當沒空。

A : Oh, what's happening?

噢，怎麼回事？

B : I have a date.

我有個約會。

A : Well, we'll make it some other time.
　　那麼，我們過些時候再說。

B : Thanks and see you around. 謝謝，再見。

Dialogue 3

A : Hi, Tom. How's it going?
　　嗨，湯姆。近況如何？

B : Fine, and yourself? 不錯，你呢？

A : Well, I'm a little short of cash right now.
　　噢，我現在稍微缺點現金。

B : Oh that's too bad. 喔，那真糟糕。

A : I was wondering if I could hit you up for a loan.
　　我想知道我是否能向你提出借錢的要求。

B : Sorry, I'd like to help you but I'm pressed for
　　money myself now.
　　抱歉，我想幫你，但是我現在手頭很緊。

〔舉一反三〕

A : Let's stop by my place for a drink.
　　咱們到我那兒去喝一杯。

B : Thanks, but I'm pressed for time tonight.
　　謝謝，但是我今晚沒空。

A : Can you help me with this project?
　　你能幫我解決這個計畫嗎？

B : No, maybe later. I'm really pressed for time.
　　不行，也許以後。我真的時間緊迫。

A : Can you give me a hand? 你能幫我個忙嗎？

B : No, I'm really under the gun.
　　不，我真的時間緊迫。

A : Can you loan me some money?
　　你能借我些錢嗎？

B : Sorry, I'm hard pressed for cash myself.
　　抱歉，我自己手頭也緊。

A : He feels he's being pressured into resigning his position.
　　他覺得他正被逼迫辭去他的職位。

B : That seems to happen when you're close to retirement.
　　在你接近退休時，那種事似乎就會發生。

《 **背景説明** 》

　　當別人問你：Can I talk to you for one minute?如果你很忙，就說：Not right now. *I'm pressed for time*. How about a little later?「不要現在，我的時間很緊迫，待會兒好嗎？」

　　用於金錢時，則表示「手頭很緊」，如：He's been out of work for three months and *he's pressed for money*.「他已經失業三個月了，手頭很緊。」

【註釋】

give sb. a hand 幫助某人
be pressed for time（*or money*）時間緊迫（金錢拮据）
stop by 順道拜訪　　*some other time* 改天；過些時候
be short of 缺乏；短少　　cash〔kæʃ〕*n.* 現金；錢
hit you up for a loan = *ask you for a loan* 向你提出借錢的請求
loan〔lon〕*n.* 借貸　*vt.* 借出　　project〔'prɑdʒɛkt〕*n.* 計畫；事業
under the gun 在槍口下，比喻「十分緊迫」
pressure〔'prɛʃɚ〕*vt.* 施以壓力；強迫　　resign〔rɪ'zaɪn〕*vt.* 辭職
position〔pə'zɪʃən〕*n.* 職位；工作　　retirement〔rɪ'taɪrmənt〕*n.* 退休

72. *I'm up to my ears in work.*

Dialogue 1

A : Good afternoon, Mrs. Green.
午安，格林太太。

B : Good afternoon, Mr. Chen. What can I do for you?
午安，陳先生。我能為你做些什麼嗎？

A : If you're free tomorrow evening, my wife and I would like to invite you to dinner.
如果你明天晚上有空，我內人和我想請你吃晚飯。

B : I'd love to come but I can't. I'm up to my ears in work.
我很願意去，但是我不能。我有非常多的工作。

A : How about Friday evening?
星期五晚上如何呢？

B : That shouldn't be any problem.
那應該沒有任何問題。

Dialogue 2

A : Let's go out for coffee.
咱們出去喝咖啡。

B : I'd like to, but I can't.
我很想去，但是我不能。

A : Why not? You've been at that desk for hours.
為何不能？你已工作很久了。

B : I'm up to my ears in work. I have to finish this report.
我的工作非常繁重。我必須完成這份報告。

A : You'd feel better if you took a break.
如果你休息一下會覺得好一點。

B : Maybe you're right. I'll go with you.
也許你是對的。我跟你一塊兒去。

Dialogue 3

A : Where's Paul? 保羅在哪兒？

B : He's still out for lunch.
他出去吃午餐還沒回來。

A : Lunch? It's two-thirty! I'm up to here with him.
午餐？兩點半了！我對他已經很生氣了。

B : He might be with a client.
他或許和某個顧客在一起。

A : I doubt it. I want to see him when he comes in.
我懷疑。當他回來時我要見他。

B : I'll tell him. 我會告訴他的。

〔舉一反三〕

A : Are you going to take a vacation?
你要休假嗎？

B : No, I can't. I'm up to my ears in work.
不，我不能。我工作十分繁重。

A : You look tired. Why don't you go home?
你看起來很疲倦。你為何不回家？

B : I can't. I'm up to my neck in work.
我沒辦法。我的工作太多了。

A : Let's go to Florida. 咱們去佛羅里達吧。

B : I wish I could. I'm behind in my work.
我希望我能去。我的工作已經落後了。

A : Let's go to the movies.
　　咱們去看電影。

B : I can't. I'm up to my elbows in dirty dishes.
　　我不能。我有很多髒盤子要洗。

A : Are you going to quit?
　　你要辭職嗎？

B : Yes. I've had this job up to here.
　　是的。我對這工作厭倦透了。

《背景說明》

　　I'm up to my ears (or neck) in work. 表示桌上要做的東西，已經堆到脖子或耳朵那麼高了，當然是非常忙碌了。這句話也可用於許多情況，如：*I'm up to my ears in* studies. 和 *I'm up to my ears in* homework.

　　另外一個形式相似，意義不同的句子是：*I'm up to here.*（說這話時要帶一個動作 —— 一隻手橫放在脖子前，手掌向下），表示「我受夠了。」意思與 *I've had enough.* 或 *I'm fed up.* 相同。

【註釋】

be up to one's ears in 沈溺於～（戀愛、工作等）中；深陷於～（困境）中而一籌莫展

be up to one's ears in work 工作繁忙

at the desk 在處理事務；在寫字　　*for hours* 一連好幾個小時

take a break 休息一下

I'm up to here with him. = *I'm angry with him.*

client〔'klaɪənt〕 *n.* 客戶

be up to one's neck in work 工作繁忙

behind〔bɪ'haɪnd〕*adv.*（工作進度）落後

be up to one's elbows 極為忙碌　　quit〔kwɪt〕*vi.,vt.* 辭職；停止

73. Where can I have this gift wrapped?

Dialogue 1

A : Will there be anything else, sir?
還有其他東西嗎？先生。

B : No, that's all.
沒有了，就這些。

A : Cash or charge?
付現金或記帳？

B : I'll pay cash. Where can I have this gift wrapped?
我付現金。我到哪兒去包裝這禮物？

A : I can do it right here if you'd like. What's the occasion?
如果你要的話我可以在這兒包裝。什麼場合用的？

B : It's my wife's birthday.
我太太的生日。

Dialogue 2

A : Where do you do gift-wrapping?
你們在哪兒包裝禮物？

B : In our service department area.
在我們的服務部門。

A : Which way is it from here?
從這兒要走哪條路？

B : Just go directly to the rear of the store.
只要直走到這家店的後面。

A : Excuse me, I'd like to have this gift wrapped.
對不起，我想要包裝這個禮物。

B : Take a ticket and wait to be called, please.
請拿一張票並等待被叫到。

Dialogue 3

A : Can I have this gift wrapped, please?
請問我能包裝這份禮物嗎？

B : Yes. What kind of paper do you want on it?
好的。你要用什麼樣的紙來包？

A : I'd like something for a man.
我要適合男人的。

B : We have two that are suitable for a man's gift. Which do you prefer?
我們有兩種適合包裝男人禮物的包裝紙。你喜歡哪一種？

A : I'll take the checked one with a dark blue ribbon.
我要那種附有一條深藍絲帶的方格紙。

B : All right. We'll have it ready in about ten minutes.
好的，大概十分鐘內就會包好。

〔舉一反三〕

A : Where can I get this gift wrapped?
我到哪兒去包裝這禮物？

B : Right this way, sir.
從這兒走，先生。

A : Where do you do gift-wrapping?
你們在哪兒包裝禮物？

B : Next to our credit office, ma'am.
在我們信用部隔壁，女士。

A : I'd like this gift wrapped, please.
　　請幫我包裝這份禮物。

B : Take a ticket and wait to be called.
　　拿一張票，並等待被叫到。

A : Would you like that gift wrapped?
　　你要包裝那份禮物嗎？

B : Yes, I certainly would.
　　是的，我當然要。

A : What's the occasion?
　　什麼場合用的？

B : It's for a baby shower.
　　是給即將分娩的母親用的。

【註釋】

　　charge〔tʃɑrdʒ〕*vi.* 記帳

　　wrap〔ræp〕*vt.* 包裝

　　gift-wrap〔'gɪft͵ræp〕*vt.* 用華麗之紙張、緞帶等包裝（禮品）

　　occasion〔ə'keʒən〕*n.* 特殊的場合

　　service department area 服務部門區

　　rear〔rɪr〕*n.* 後部；背部

　　suitable〔'sutəbl̩〕*adj.* 適合的

　　checked〔tʃɛkt〕*adj.* 方格子花紋的

　　ribbon〔'rɪbən〕*n.* 絲帶；緞帶

　　baby shower 指「送禮物給即將分娩的母親的集會」

74. You took the words right out of my mouth.

Dialogue 1

A : This food looks great.
這食物看起來很棒。

B : Yes, I can't wait to try it.
是的，我等不及要嚐它。

A : Mmmm, this is the best steak I've ever eaten.
嗯，這是我所吃過的最好的牛排。

B : You took the words right out of my mouth.
你說的跟我要說的一樣。

A : I never thought it would be this good.
我從沒想到它會這麼好。

B : I should tell Bob about this place. I know he'd love it.
我應告訴鮑伯這個地方。我知道他會喜歡它的。

Dialogue 2

A : This restaurant is awful.
這家餐廳眞糟。

B : It sure is. Even the menu is dirty.
的確是。連菜單也是髒的。

A : I can't believe Mac recommended this place.
我無法相信麥克推薦這地方。

B : Me, either.
我也是。

A : Let's get out of here.
　　我們離開這裏吧。

B : You took the words right out of my mouth.
　　你說了我要說的話。

Dialogue 3

A : Is that Randy's girlfriend?
　　那是藍迪的女朋友嗎？

B : Yes. I met her yesterday.
　　是的。我昨天見過她。

A : She's gorgeous!
　　她真是美極了！。

B : She sure is.
　　她的確是。

A : I wonder what she sees in Randy.
　　我想知道她眼中的藍迪是什麼樣子。

B : You took the words right out of my mouth.
　　你說出了我正要說的話。

〔舉一反三〕

A : This movie is terrible. Let's leave.
　　這部電影真難看。咱們走吧。

B : You took the words right out of my mouth.
　　你說了我正要說的話。

A : This party is boring.
　　這個宴會真無聊。

B : You took the words right out of my mouth.
　　你搶了我要說的話。

A : I think it's time for a coffee break.
　　我想該是喝咖啡休息的時候了。

B : You took the words right out of my mouth.
　　你說了我正要說的話。

A : The water looks good. Let's go for a boat ride.
　　這水看起來真美。咱們搭船去兜風。

B : I was just about to suggest that.
　　我剛好要那樣建議。

A : I think it's too cold to go swimming.
　　我想天氣太冷不能游泳。

B : I was just going to say that.
　　我正要那樣說。

【註釋】

take the words out of one's mouth 搶先說出某人想要說的話

awful〔'ɔfḷ〕*adj.* 可怕的；極壞的

menu〔'mɛnju〕*n.* 菜單

recommend〔‚rɛkə'mɛnd〕*vt.* 介紹；推薦

gorgeous〔'gɔrdʒəs〕*adj.* 華麗的；好看的

boring〔'borɪŋ〕*adj.* 無聊的

a coffee break 喝咖啡的休息時間

a boat ride 指坐船，著重在乘坐，而非由自己控制。

75. *I'd like to have this prescription filled.*

Dialogue 1

A : Your ear is infected. I'll prescribe some antibiotics for you. That should clear it up.

你的耳朵受感染了。我開一些抗生素給你。那會把你耳朵的細菌清除掉。

B : Thank you, Doctor.

謝謝你,醫生。

(*at the drugstore* 在藥房)

A : May I help you?

我能幫助你嗎?

B : Yes, I'd like to have this prescription filled.

是的,我要照這藥方配藥。

A : O.K. I'll have it for you right away.

好的。我馬上替你弄。

B : Thanks.

謝謝。

Dialogue 2

A : I'd like to have this prescription filled.

我要照這份藥方配藥。

B : All right. Let me see if we have it in stock.

好的。讓我看看我們有沒有現貨供應。

A : Please do. The doctor said that it might be hard to fill.

請看看。醫生說這藥可能很難配到。

B : Yes, we do have it.

有的,我們有貨。

A : Oh, good. When will it be ready?

噢，好。什麼時候可以弄好？

B : We should have it for you in about five minutes.

大概五分鐘內我們會把它替你弄好。

Dialogue 3

A : What's wrong with you?

你怎麼回事？

B : Well, I've been running a fever and I have a sore throat.

噢，我發燒而且喉嚨痛。

A : Let's take a look at your throat.

讓我們瞧瞧你的喉嚨。

B : It's so sore I can hardly swallow.

它痛得我幾乎不能吞嚥。

A : I'll give you a prescription that you can have filled at your local drugstore.

我給你開張藥方。你可以在你們當地的藥局買到。

B : Thank you. 謝謝你。

〔舉一反三〕

A : I'd like to have this prescription filled, please.

請幫我照這藥方配藥。

B : All right. It'll take a few minutes.

好的。那需要一些時間。

A : I'd like this prescription filled, please.

我要照這份藥方配藥。

B : Certainly. It'll be ready shortly.

當然可以。很快就會準備好。

A : Can I have this prescription filled, please?
　　我能照這份藥方配藥嗎？

B : Yes. We'll call you when it's ready.
　　可以的。準備好後我們會叫你。

A : He had to have two cavities filled today.
　　他今天有兩個牙洞必須補滿。

B : I'll bet that was no fun.
　　我相信那並不好玩。

A : I have to fill the car with gasoline.
　　我必須把這輛車子的汽油加滿。

B : It's certainly expensive to run a car these days.
　　現在開車一定很貴。

【註釋】

infect (ɪn'fɛkt) *vt.* 傳染；感染
prescribe (prɪ'skraɪb) *vt.* 開藥方
antibiotics (‚æntɪbaɪ'ɑtɪks) *n. pl.* 抗生素
drugstore ('drʌg‚stor) *n.* （美）藥房；雜貨店
prescription (prɪ'skrɪpʃən) *n.* 藥方
fill a prescription 照藥方配藥
in stock 備有；持有；現貨供應
run a fever 發燒
sore (sor, sɔr) *adj.* 疼痛的
throat (θrot) *n.* 喉嚨
cavity ('kævətɪ) *n.* 穴；洞；蛀牙洞
these days 這些日子；最近

76. Can I try this on?

Dialogue 1

A : May I help you?
我能幫忙你嗎?

B : Yes, please. I'm looking for a trench coat.
是的,我正在找一件有腰帶的雙層雨衣。

A : What size do you need?
你需要什麼樣的尺碼?

B : 37 regular. 普通37號的。

A : How do you like this one?
你喜歡這一件嗎?

B : It looks nice. Can I try this on?
它看來很好。我能試穿嗎?

Dialogue 2

A : I need some pants.
我需要一些褲子。

B : What size do you take?
你穿多大尺寸的?

A : A 32 waist and a 35 length.
32腰圍和35褲長的。

B : How do you like this pair?
你喜歡這條嗎?

A : They look fine. Can I try them on?
看起來不錯。我能試穿看看嗎?

B : Sure. The dressing room is right over there.
當然。更衣室就那兒。

Dialogue 3

A : Can I help you?
我能幫忙你嗎？

B : Yes. I'm interested in a pair of jeans for my son.
好的。我想替我兒子買條牛仔褲。

A : Do you know what size he wears?
你知道他穿多大尺寸的？

B : Well, he's between sizes right now.
嗯，他現在什麼尺寸都不適合。

A : You're welcome to exchange them for another size if they don't fit.
如果不合適的話，歡迎你來換其他尺寸。

B : All right. Thank you.
好的，謝謝你。

〔舉一反三〕

A : Can I try this on?
我能試穿這件嗎？

B : Sure. The dressing room is right here.
當然。更衣室就在這兒。

A : May I try this on?
我能試穿這件嗎？

B : Yes, the changing room is right over there.
可以的，更衣室就在那兒。

A : Can I try these dresses on?
我能試穿這些衣服嗎？

B : Yes, the fitting room is this way.
可以的，更衣室這兒走。

A : Can I exchange this if it doesn't fit?
　　如果不合適的話我能換嗎？

B : Yes, but be sure to keep your receipt and return it within ten days.
　　可以的，但是不要忘記保留收據，同時要在十天內退回。

A : I need to exchange this for a different size.
　　我需要換一件不同尺寸的。

B : Certainly. What size do you need?
　　當然。你需要多大的尺寸？

【註釋】

　　trench coat 1. 指一種有腰帶的軍用防水短上衣。　2. 有腰帶和肩帶的厚雨衣
　　3. 一種有腰帶的雙層雨衣。

　　regular〔ˈrɛgjələ〕*n.* 普通尺寸的現成衣服

　　try on 試穿

　　waist〔west〕*n.* 腰

　　dressing room, changing room, fitting room 都指「更衣室」。

　　jeans〔dʒinz〕*n. pl.* 牛仔褲

　　fit〔fɪt〕*vi.* 合適

　　exchange〔ɪksˈtʃendʒ〕*vt.* 交換；互換

　　receipt〔rɪˈsit〕*n.* 收據

77. *Just to be on the safe side.*

Dialogue 1

A : Did you say you're taking Susan out tonight?
你說你今天晚上要帶蘇珊出去嗎？

B : Yes, we're going to the Red Fox for dinner.
是的，我們要去「紅狐」吃晚餐。

A : Do you have enough money?
你有足夠的錢嗎？

B : Forty dollars, why? 四十元，幹嘛？

A : You didn't hear? She eats a lot.
難道你沒聽說？她吃得很多。

B : I didn't know that. I'd better take sixty dollars just to be on the safe side.
我不知道。爲安全起見我最好帶六十元。

Dialogue 2

A : Are you going out? 你要出去嗎？

B : Yes. I think I'll take a walk. Want to join me?
是的。我想我要去散步。要不要跟我一塊兒去？

A : No. I think I'll stay in and read.
不。我想我將待在家裏看書。

B : That sky looks a little cloudy.
天空看來有點烏雲。

A : Yes, it does. It looks like rain.
是的。好像要下雨了。

B : Just to be on the safe side, I'll take an umbrella with me. 爲了安全起見，我要帶支雨傘。

Dialogue 3

A : Hello, Jane. Do you have my tickets?
　　哈囉，珍。妳拿到了我的機票嗎？

B : Yes. You're on Flight 201 leaving at seven-thirty tonight.
　　是的。你搭今天晚上 7 點 30 分起飛的 201 班機。

A : Good. What about the return trip tickets?
　　好。回程機票如何？

B : I made the reservations, but just to be on the safe side, you should reconfirm them.
　　我已經預訂了，但是為了安全起見，你最好再確定一下。

A : I'll do that when I arrive in Los Angeles.
　　當我到達洛杉磯時我會那樣做的。

B : Have a good trip.
　　祝旅途愉快。

〔舉一反三〕

A : Did you turn off the TV?
　　你關掉電視了嗎？

B : Yes, I did, but just to be on the safe side, I pulled out the plug from the wall.
　　是的，我關了，但是為了安全起見，我拔掉牆上的插頭。

A : Are you sure the campfire is out?
　　你確定營火熄了？

B : Yes, I am, but just to be on the safe side, I poured water on it.
　　是的，我確定，但是為了安全起見，我在上面倒了水。

A : It's chilly tonight.

今晚有點冷。

B : I thought it might be, so just to be safe, I brought my jacket.

我想可能會這樣，所以為了安全起見，我帶了夾克。

A : This bill is expensive.

這筆帳費用龐大。

B : That's okay. Just to be on the safe side, I brought some extra money.

那沒關係。為了安全起見，我帶了些額外的錢。

A : Are you sure your bicycle is O.K. there?

你確定你的腳踏車在那裏很安全？

B : Yes, but I locked it just to be on the safe side.

是的，但是為安全起見，我把它鎖了。

【註釋】

to be on the safe side 為安全起見；以防萬一

join〔dʒɔɪn〕*vt.* 加入

stay in 留在家裏；不出門

reservation〔ˌrɛzəˈveʃən〕*n.* （房間、座位、門票等的）預訂

reconfirm〔ˌrikənˈfɝm〕*vt.* 再確認

turn off 關閉（電視、收音機）；扭熄（燈光）；關掉（煤氣、自來水）

pull out 拔掉

plug〔plʌg〕*n.* 插頭

campfire〔ˈkæmpˌfaɪr〕*n.* 營火

pour〔por, pɔr〕*vt.* 倒；澆；灌

chilly〔ˈtʃɪlɪ〕*adj.* （指天氣）頗冷的；寒冷的

jacket〔ˈdʒækɪt〕*n.* 夾克

78. *I hope I didn't offend you.*

Dialogue 1

A : How old are you?
你幾歲了？

B : How old do you think I am?
你認為我幾歲？

A : I'd say you're about 35.
我說你大概三十五歲。

B : No, I'm only 29!
不，我只有二十九歲！

A : Oh, I'm sorry. I hope I didn't offend you.
噢，我很抱歉。希望我沒使你生氣。

B : That's all right, but I think you need glasses.
那沒關係，不過我想你需要眼鏡。

Dialogue 2

A : You speak English without an accent. Where did you learn it?
你說英語時沒有口音。你在哪裏學的？

B : I'm an American. 我是個美國人。

A : Oh, I'm sorry. I hope I didn't offend you.
噢，我很抱歉。希望我沒有使你生氣。

B : It's O.K. 沒關係。

A : Were you born and raised in the States?
你是在美國土生土長的嗎？

B : No. My family came to America when I was about five. 不。我大約五歲時我的家人來到美國。

Dialogue 3

A : Did you change your hairstyle?
　　你改變了你的髮型嗎？

B : Yes, I did.
　　是的，我改了。

A : I liked it better the other way.
　　我比較喜歡原來的樣子。

B : Well, I wanted to try something different.
　　噢，我想試試不同的樣子。

A : Oh, I hope I didn't offend you.
　　喔，我希望我沒有使你生氣。

B : That's all right. You're entitled to your own opinion.
　　那沒關係。你有權表示你的意見。

〔舉一反三〕

A : I'm sorry if you can't understand my English.
　　如果你無法了解我的英文，我很抱歉。

B : I hope I didn't offend you.
　　我希望我沒有使你生氣。

A : I'm not 35, I'm only 29 years old.
　　我不是三十五歲，我只有二十九歲。

B : Oh, I hope I didn't hurt your feelings.
　　噢，我希望我沒有傷了你的心。

A : Are you saying you don't like my new hairstyle?
　　你是說你不喜歡我的新髮型嗎？

B : I hope I didn't offend you.
　　我希望我沒有使妳生氣。

A : So you don't like the way I do things.
　　你不喜歡我做事的方法。
B : I didn't mean to offend you.
　　我不是故意要使你生氣。

A : Am I boring you with my work?
　　我的工作是不是使你厭煩？
B : Sorry, I didn't mean to offend you.
　　抱歉，我不是故意要使你生氣的。

【註釋】

offend〔ə'fɛnd〕vt. 觸怒；傷～感情；使生氣
accent〔'æksɛnt〕n. 腔調；口音
raise〔rez〕vt. 養育
entitle〔ɪn'taɪtl̩〕vt. 使有資格；使有權利
mean to 故意；蓄意

79. *How often do you work out?*

Dialogue 1

A : You're looking very well.
　　妳看起來非常好。

B : Thank you. I try to keep in shape.
　　謝謝你。我試著保持身材。

A : How often do you work out?
　　你多久做一次運動？

B : Every other day.
　　每隔一天。

A : Do you jog?
　　你慢跑嗎？

B : Yes, but I also work out at a health club.
　　是的，不過我也在健身俱樂部做運動練習。

Dialogue 2

A : You look like you've lost weight.
　　你看起來好像體重減輕了。

B : I have. I lost ten pounds exercising.
　　我是的。我運動減去了十磅。

A : No wonder you look so good. How often do you work out?
　　難怪你看起來這麼棒。你多久做一次運動？

B : I jog thirty minutes every morning and then I lift weights in the afternoon.
　　我每天早上慢跑三十分鐘，然後下午我舉重。

A : I think I'm going to start working out.
　　我想我要開始運動了。

B : You really should. It makes you feel a lot better.
　　你真的應該運動。它使你感覺好很多。

Dialogue 3

A : Tom is in great shape, isn't he?
　　湯姆身材很好，不是嗎？

B : He sure is.
　　他的確是。

A : How often does he work out?
　　他多久運動一次？

B : Five times a week from what I hear.
　　我聽說一個星期五次。

A : I wonder how he finds the time.
　　我真想知道他如何找到時間的。

B : I don't know, but it's paid off for him.
　　我不知道，不過他總算是有收穫。

〔舉一反三〕

A : How often do you work out?
　　你多久做一次運動？

B : At least twice a week.
　　至少一星期兩次。

A : Where have you been?
　　你到哪去了？

B : At the health club. I was working out.
　　在健身俱樂部。我在運動。

A : I'm really out of shape.

我真的沒有什麼身材。

B : You need to work out at the gym.

你需要在體育館運動。

A : That fighter has a good build.

那名拳擊手有很好的體格。

B : Yes. He's really in shape.

是的，他真的身材不錯。

A : You're looking good.

你現在看來不錯。

B : Thanks. I try to keep in shape.

謝謝。我試著保持身材。

【註釋】

work out 運動

in shape 身材良好合宜

out of shape 身材不好

jog〔dʒɑg〕*vi.* 慢跑

health club 健身中心；健身俱樂部

pound〔paʊnd〕*n.* 磅（1磅＝0.45359公斤）

lift〔lɪft〕*vt.* 舉起　*lift weights* 舉重

be paid off 有代價；得到收穫

twice〔twaɪs〕*adv.* 兩次

gym〔dʒɪm〕*n.* 體育館（為 gymnasium〔dʒɪmˈneziəm〕的縮寫）

build〔bɪld〕*n.* 體格

80. *How long have you been in the States?*

Dialogue 1

A : You speak English without an accent. How did you learn to speak English so well?
你說英文沒有口音。你學說英文怎麼學得這麼好？

B : Thank you. I've studied it since I was in junior high.
謝謝你。我從初中就開始學了。

A : Oh, how long have you been in the States?
噢，你來美國多久了？

B : About ten years.
大約十年。

A : Is your family here, too?
你的家人也在這兒嗎？

B : Yes, all of them are here except my sister.
是的，除了我姊姊外都在這兒。

Dialogue 2

A : When will you be leaving for the United States?
你何時要去美國？

B : Next Friday.
下星期五。

A : Friday? Why are you leaving so soon?
星期五？你為何那麼快就要去？

B : I have to enroll in school next Thursday.
我必須在下個星期四登記入學。

A : How long will you stay in California?

你在加利福尼亞要待多久？

B : Just for one year. I'm only going there to study English.

只有一年，我只是要去那裏學英文。

Dialogue 3

A : How long has Chris been working here?

克里斯在這兒工作多久了？

B : Oh, a long time —— at least ten years.

噢，很久了—— 至少十年。

A : Did he start right after college?

他大學一畢業就開始在那裡工作嗎？

B : Yes. He started out as a clerk.

是的，他從一個辦事員開始做起。

A : He's done very well, hasn't he?

他做得相當好，不是嗎？

B : Yes. He should be a manager soon.

是的。他應該快成為一個經理了。

〔舉一反三〕

A : How long have you been in the States?

你在美國待多久了？

B : Two years. I'll return to Taiwan next June.

兩年。我明年六月回台灣。

A : Have you been in the States long?

你在美國待了很久嗎？

B : I've lived here for five years.

我在這裏住了五年了。

A : How long have you been waiting for the bus?
　　你等巴士等了多久？
B : About half an hour.
　　大概半個小時。

A : How long will you be in the library?
　　你要在圖書館待多久？
B : All day. I have to study.
　　整天。我必須讀書。

A : Are you going to be long?
　　你要去很久嗎？
B : No, only about ten minutes. Wait for me.
　　不，只要大概十分鐘。等我。

【註釋】

junior (ˈdʒunjɚ) *adj.* 年少的 ↔ senior (ˈsinjɚ) *adj.* 年長的
junior high 初中（senior high 高中）
the States = the United States 美國
leave for 離開（此地）前往…
enroll (ɪnˈrol) *vi.* 登記（姓名）；註冊
Chris (krɪs) *n.* 克里斯
clerk (klɝk) *n.* 辦事員；售貨員；店員
manager (ˈmænɪdʒɚ) *n.* 經理

Editorial Staff

● **編譯** / 張 齡

● **校訂** / 劉 毅・謝靜芳・吳凱琳・蔡琇瑩・高瑋謙

● **校閱** / David Lightle ・ Bruce S. Stewart

● **封面設計** / 張鳳儀

● **美編** / 張鳳儀・蕭寶雲

● **打字** / 黃淑貞・吳秋香・蘇淑玲

All rights reserved. No part of this publication may be reproduced without the prior permission of Learning Publishing Company.

本書版權爲學習出版公司所有，翻印必究。

||||||||||||| ●學習出版公司門市部● |||||||||||||||

台北地區：台北市許昌街 10 號 2 樓 TEL：(02)2331-4060・2331-9209
台中地區：台中市綠川東街 32 號 8 樓 23 室
　　　　　TEL：(04)223-2838

|||||||||||||||||||||||||||||||||||||||||||||||||

五分鐘學會說英文 ③

編　　譯 / 張　齡
發 行 所 / 學習出版有限公司　　　　　☎ (02) 2704-5525
郵 撥 帳 號 / 0512727-2 學習出版社帳戶
登 記 證 / 局版台業 2179 號
印 刷 所 / 裕強彩色印刷有限公司
台 北 門 市 / 台北市許昌街 10 號 2 F　　☎ (02) 2331-4060・2331-9209
台 中 門 市 / 台中市綠川東街 32 號 8 F 23 室　☎ (04) 223-2838
台灣總經銷 / 紅螞蟻圖書有限公司　　　☎ (02) 2799-9490・2657-0132
美國總經銷 / Evergreen Book Store　　☎ (818) 2813622

售價：新台幣一百八十元正
2000 年 2 月 1 日二版一刷

ISBN 957-519-080-7
版權所有・翻印必究